Maternal Instincts

SM Thomas

Written by:
SM Thomas

Published by:
A.R Hurne Publishing

Edited by:
Allison Reinert, A Favorite Pen

Cover Art by:
Germancreative – Les

ISBN
978-1-7396769-7-1

DEDICATION

For Mum – thank you for never leading a real-life cult
or trying to kill my husband x

Definition:

Maternal Instinct

In British English

NOUN:

The natural tendency that a mother has
to behave or react in a particular way around her child or
children.

Out of all the safe houses we move through, this one is my least favourite. It's not the house itself that offends me, it contains the same bland furniture we have in every safe house. A rickety sofa, three well-worn beds, blank walls devoid of personality, and a shower that only really works for half an hour first thing in the morning. My reason for disliking this house most of all wasn't materialistic, in fact I'd grown quite accustomed to living a simpler life. The only item of value I had in my possession was a laptop and even that had seen better days. And truth be told, I've always been a minimalist, a 'less is more' kind of person. Granted, my less used to cost a lot more than the surroundings I now spend my days in but beggars can't be choosers.

No, it's not the house itself that's the problem. It's the location.

It's positioned directly behind the battlefield, right next to the firing line. I never sleep deeply for the seven days we're stationed here and it's impossible to get any work done with the surrounding noise of weapons and death. I simply can't relax in the eye of such chaos. All I can do is sit around and think or make small talk with Georgia and Ryle, something that's become less appealing as the years have rolled on. It's not that I dislike them, more that I've learnt to keep them at arm's length. After what happened to Violet I have no other choice. I'm not sure I could survive another wave of grief like that.

efficient sweep, I managed it on my wedding day. I should never have attacked Jack. I should have been smarter than that. More in control. Less emotional.

If I hadn't attacked him, then my mother would never have guessed that I knew about her involvement in our accident or that I knew she was trying to steal the disease from the Dwellers. What other reason would I have to try and kill her husband? No doubt he sang like a canary to her after he awoke.

She was hunting me just like everybody else. Her fear would come true - that if I somehow got the Dwellers to listen without killing me, then she would lose the strongest ally she had. If they knew she exploited their DNA too it would be over for her. No longer queen of the movement. Di couldn't allow that to happen even if it meant silencing her daughter. She may have tried to save me when Jack shot at our car, but now she was out for my blood just as much as anyone.

For survival, we were reliant on a small pocket of sympathisers from both sides of the war. There were a handful of Dwellers who had agreed not to seek vengeance for their fallen loved ones because of my connection to Kyan. Eventually, they believed what I told them. That it had been the State that had slaughtered their friends and family to create a disease. My mother wanted to use the virus to create her own super soldiers. That Leo, Violet, and I were just pawns in their plan.

Violet.

the border, but they did still exist. They helped us move undetected every week between safe houses. It was a ballache but necessary and the only way to keep the three of us out of harm's way. A week was just about long enough before witnesses to our presence started asking questions. They whispered, wondering who we were and what we were doing moving into their area.

Our faces were plastered everywhere as the State's 'most wanted' and although we changed our appearances, if you stared at us long enough, it was still painfully obvious who we were. Short of under-the-counter surgery, your face would always be your face.

Georgia had taken to standing outside in the light of the Suns more often, taking the porcelain edge from her skin. She now had a neat row of freckles from ear to ear. They mostly congregated around her nose, it suited her. They softened her face and made her look years younger, especially without the makeup she used to apply every day painstakingly. She cut her long hair and dyed it a dark non-descript shade of brown. Out of the three of us, she was the least recognisable nowadays. She'd barely pass for an Agent Cherry impersonator. Unlike Georgia, Ryle and I stayed away from the Suns as much as possible. The melanin in our skin didn't need any further encouragement.

Ryle had made the tough decision to shave his head shortly after our escape. I watched his face from behind my wall of grief as the locs he'd been so proud of fell to the floor at his feet. His hair was one of the most recognisable things about him, but I knew he had not

But during his campaign he made a point of keeping his locs, despite what some early articles wrote about him. In doing so had hoped he'd change even the smallest of minds. One early interviewer had described his hair as looking as though it would smell like patchouli oil and weed. A hideously small minded, racist and outdated way of looking at the world. Thankfully as Ryle's popularity grew that journalist's career plummeted, until he was nothing more than a footnote in the history of our Settlement. Karma can still exist in this world of ours.

As I listened to him turn off the razor and take a deep breath, I knew he was saying goodbye to that life. If anything, being associated with criminals like us would only compound the small-minded beliefs that still lingered in the populous. The State may lead with the story that he had been kidnapped by the two of us, but there would always be those out there that doubted his innocence. I didn't know if he'd ever be able to shake their mistrust after this.

I'd taken the razor and scissors from Ryle shortly after he'd finished. I sat on the floor with my legs crossed and looked at myself in the mirror. My curls were so long now, and they seemed even darker than before because of the lack of sunshine in the last two months. My mother had always loved my hair growing up. She'd taken the time to teach me to care for it properly and some weekends she'd spend hours painstakingly braiding what felt like each strand into an hands and was able to fashion what remained of my hair into a passable pixie cut, but the damage had been done. The beautiful curls I loved and loathed in equal measures for so many years were gone. A piece of me that my mother had loved so truly was gone.

Good.

Sometimes we had a vehicle to help us move, but more often than not we had to abscond from the safety of our house to the next on foot. There was no apparent rhyme or pattern as to which house we moved to. Sometimes we'd be back at the same one within eight weeks, whilst others we wouldn't see again for nearly a year. I assumed Ryle had an overall plan for our movements, but more often than not, it felt like he was half-arsing it.

Ryle. My husband. A man who I was slowly beginning to once again consider a friend. It had taken me two months after Violet's funeral to calm down enough to listen to him. I sat, now drained of all emotion, as he explained the countless assumptions I had about him. How it had been his father who had forged his signature on the document about Franklin's parental rights. How it had been Bailey's idea for him to agree to the plan for us to be the next rulers of the State. It had made him untouchable as far as Paul was concerned, which is why he stood up to him when he attacked Violet. It's why he'd been able to get Jack invited to the birthday party and wedding, and it was why he could ensure our escape plan worked. He only undercover in their camp, feeding us information as she was able. It's how we've avoided being captured by them for the last two years. Georgia missed Lizzie Terribly. I could see it on her face every time one of her messages arrived. They were supposed to be living together happily ever after, but Lizzie had known all along that wouldn't be possible. She knew she was never part of the contingency plan that we were all now living.

I didn't know how Georgia wasn't angry at her, but when Ryle explained the situation and all that Lizzie had done for us, she simply nodded her head and said that she understood. Lizzie was being an excellent agent. I guess rationalising it as a professional obligation rather than a choice must make it easier to stomach.

I suppose it was the same way in which I rationalised the video that Violet had been forced to narrate. I understood exactly what threats they would have placed upon her to coerce her into complying. I knew every word she'd been forced to speak would have killed her and that being unable to warn us would have tortured her everyday. But what choice did she have? They had her child. A mother should do everything she can to protect her child. It's been two years, but they still play that broadcast nightly; a way to make sure that everybody still hates us. Her voice still haunts me whenever I catch snippets of it floating through the evening air. I should have guessed Paul had a backup plan when she went missing. I should have pressed her more when she returned. Maybe I could have saved her.

storm rages. Even Dwellers try to avoid the boiling rain. I'm used to the sting of it now though. My hands are covered in blisters that heal just in time for me to be hit by new drops as we move between homes. We can't wait around for storms to clear. I suppose it's easy to live with the pain of a burn when you know people are waiting to tear you limb from limb if you stumble or move slowly on a journey.

So once in a grey moon, I get the chance to use actual equipment, to analyse the sample Rus stole for me all those years ago, and to test any theories I've dreamt up. The rest of the time is spent piecing together what I know in a Word document on my laptop. It's a painfully slow process, and I've asked Ryle more than once if we can just stay in the house near the lab for a couple of months. If I had a solid run at this, then I knew I could cure the disease. We could save so many people if he would just let me stay still. I've even offered to stay behind on my own, minimising the risk to him and Georgia.

But he never does. He always points out that the cure will never be finished if I get captured or killed. I always concede to that point. And we always move on. My job is to find a cure, his job is to keep us alive.

He explained more about the so-called Architects or the Téssera over our many months together. I guess we ran out of conversation one night because suddenly the truth came spilling out of him. Regina's dad had been one. So had Ryle's grandfather. The four men who orchestrated the human race's escape from a dying intentions weren't the best when everybody who knew about their work fell sick or had accidents during the first year of the Settlement. Looking back in the history books it was described as the year of misfortune brought about by trouble adjusting to the new landscape. But as far as I'm aware, no sickness or accident causes ligature marks around your neck.

Eventually, whispers of the Téssera became nothing more than folklore and the name disappeared altogether. That's when people switched to referring to them as the Architects and, by people, I mean conspiracy theorists. Who would have thought they would be right about this one?

Every decision the State made, every bit of independence we thought we had over our lives was a lie. Anything and everything was decided by four people in one room. The President and all the differing political parties were nothing more than a curtain for them to hide behind. Democracy existed only in their board room, not shared amongst the general populous despite appearances.

When the original members passed away, their seat at the table was given to their most promising offspring. Regina had turned hers down. I had an even deeper respect for the woman after hearing that. She chose to marry William and run the hospital instead, wanting to distance herself from her father's controlling power. It meant that the seat was still vacant. Would they have offered it to Leo eventually? Would they offer it to Franklin?

on the safe arrival of her grandson, they had already fled. They live in a tiny house tucked safely away from the border in Dweller territory. Ada and her dad live next door. I've seen Franklin from a distance a handful of times over the last two years. He's so big now. Three whole years old. He now moves with confidence and although I can't hear his words, I can tell that he's already capable of holding a conversation. Rus always seems enthralled by whatever Franklin is telling him. Every time I sneak across the border to watch them, I have to resist the maternal pull to go to him. I know Rus will have told him all about me and Leo. He wouldn't let him forget who his parents were. Are.

Ryle pretends he doesn't know I sneak out to see my son when we're in the safe house nearby. But he's always packed up and ready to move when I return. I know it's the biggest risk I could take. There's no doubt the Dwellers that aren't on our side will be watching that house like a hawk, but I can't resist. And he knows that. I see the look of relief on his face each time I return undetected.

Georgia wants to destroy the Tésseras for all that they've done to us. All that they've done to humanity. I can't say I disagree with her, but right now my focus needs to be on the cure. People will be more likely to listen to our story if we can promise them they will be okay. Until we have public opinion back on our side, we can't hope to wage a war against the elite. Other than Ryle's dad we don't even know who fills the other three seats. Ryle does not know who, if anyone, stepped in for

Once I had that, we could take on the world.

If you can believe it, life in the Settlement has got worse over the last two years. It took the State six months after our escape to put their actual plans into action under the guise of, once again, protecting people.

They built a new school, one specifically for children who had been highlighted as being affected by the disease they had created. Children highlighted to them, in part, by the 'death test' I'd built with Violet. The lucky ones who wouldn't be killed by the disease, but who showed promise of change once infected. These children were kept within school grounds twenty-four hours a day, seven days a week, with no contact with the outside world. They were cut off from friends and family and nobody truly knew what went on behind closed doors. I could hazard a guess but didn't like to. They were children. I had to tell myself that the State wouldn't hurt children the way they hurt me, no matter how loud my instincts screamed at me. I knew better than that.

Of course, the State made sure the Newsies ran positive stories about the education the children were receiving and the feats they had achieved in their short time within the grounds. They were all excelling in their studies; achieving grades that the children in the normal State schools could only dream of.

Babies were tested immediately after birth to see what their chances were at surviving the disease, taking them from the post-natal ward if they were found to possess the ability to develop superhuman powers. I couldn't imagine how those mothers felt, only hours given free medical care for all household members. Suddenly average illnesses and sicknesses could become a thing of the past, no longer things to fear or live with, and all you had to do was hand over that one child who was special. That sacrifice could one day lead to the survival of any less fortunate children you had under your care should the worst happen to them.

I knew, as a mother, that wouldn't be enough to sway me. But I also knew that I had a level of privilege few of my fellow parents had. As the son of the leading researcher for the Settlement, and as the grandson set to inherit his grandmother's hospital, Franklin would never have been in danger of dying from anything as straightforward as heart disease. He would have been treated free of charge, at the first murmur of something wrong.

Franklin would always be looked after in that regard. Medically he would always be safe thanks to me. And thanks to my connection to Kyan and my friendship with Violet, he would always be safe on Dweller land.

The Helsas would always care for him and as long as they remained the leading tribe amongst the Dwellers, he would always be safe. Violet's ex-husband, Tendai, had made sure that Rus, Theo, and Franklin were given a home just across from their own. That way they could monitor the child that Violet had considered a nephew. He wanted every one of his followers to know that the child was protected by him personally. It was the best way to ensure his safety. I knew that there were many

I'd believed their lie that all I had to do was marry Ryle to achieve my freedom. In reality, they'd set me up to become the wife of the President as a way to keep me as their puppet for the rest of my life. They were still running with the lie that Ryle had been kidnapped. I guess all the witnesses who had seen him running hand in hand with us towards the escape van had been dealt with.

There was no one around to refute their claims that the President-in-waiting was being held hostage somewhere unknown by two terrorists. They were officially calling him that now - the President-in-waiting. Public response to the title had been positive. Ryle had already been a popular political figure before our wedding and the idea that I had both broken his heart and stolen him from society had only further cemented the Settlements' love for him. Currently, the State lives under a caretaker President. Not much was known about him. Truth be told, I doubted his existence. He was just a smoke screen to disguise the fact that the Téssera were now pulling the strings directly; a way to keep the belief in democracy alive.

Bailey fed us these stories via the supporters who helped us move from house to house. Sometimes they even came with newspaper clippings. At least if I saw it in print I knew it was the reality being fed to the Settlement. Bailey herself never came to visit. It was too risky, Ryle explained. She had to stay as far under the radar as possible in order to keep aiding our efforts. I had a feeling my mother wasn't even aware of the fact between safe houses. He was the one who had access to the lab and had a keen interest in helping me find the cure. Ruland kept to himself. He had exchanged a few friendly words with Ryle but he kept his distance from us as best he could. I got the feeling that he didn't fully believe in our innocence; there was uncertainty to him. He was the weak spot in our armour as far as I was concerned, so I treated him with the same indifference he showed me and relied on Elijio for my updates from the Dweller side of the planet.

Elijio was the one who kept me aware of Franklin's progress and safety, who told me that slowly but surely the Dwellers were questioning the State's story about us and the disease. A whisper here, a whisper there and one day the Dwellers would be on our side. I was sure of it. It just took time to change opinions but thankfully time was all I had these days. If Ryle would just let me stay with Elijio then I knew the two of us could create a cure with a month of solid work and research. But he never listened to my reason. Sometimes when we were travelling with Elijio I fantasised about running away with him. He could keep me hidden. Ryle and Georgia would have to forgive me when I finally removed the scrutiny and hatred that had been placed upon us two years ago. They would have to. But I never ran, I never escaped. I had lost the fire in my belly after what had happened to Violet.

Carla was a talkative creature. I could always rely on her to fill me in on the information that Bailey had left out. Sometimes the information was nothing more her.

So, they'd moved ahead with their plan to force us all into breeding, controlling us once again under the guise of ensuring the survival of the human race. People like Carla were unhappy with the decision. She was in her early twenties and had only been married for six months. She'd hoped to live her life for a few more years before having children. Something she was more than entitled to lust after. She told me she was almost relieved that she still hadn't fallen pregnant eighteen months after being forced into giving up her birth control. However, if they hit the two-year mark she and her husband would both be 'invited' to a fertility clinic to make sure they were doing all they could to help the repopulation efforts. None of her situation was fair and yet she still smiled as we traipsed through woodlands towards our next safe house. She was like Ryle, someone who always tried to focus on the sunnier side of life.

Ryle laughed a lot less these days than he had when we'd first met. The joy in him had slowly been eaten away by the last two years. I noticed it after we lost Violet. Seeing somebody die in front of you can do that to a person, especially when that person dies so violently. I was used to seeing the light disappear from someone's eyes. I'd witnessed it enough times as a Doctor and snuffed it out from my eyes. I can pinpoint the moment though where he stopped trying to see the good in the world. It was when Bailey sent us news of the abortion ban. The one thing Ryle had been so all the future children who would have to grow up with the guilt that their life came at the cost of their mothers'. Children like him.

Carla told us about the handful of people in the central zones who had tried to fight the ban. They created signs and chants and moved towards the Government's court to make their displeasure known. They all disappeared that day, never to be heard from or spoken about again. Their families never lodged a missing person case, no police files were created and no publicly recorded executions were carried out. Twenty people just vanished. And everybody was okay with it. Everyone just carried on as though it hadn't happened. As though the State hadn't swept up a handful of citizens and murdered them to silence them.

I nearly told Ryle that we could go back to the Settlement that day. I could see in his body language that all he wanted to do was return back and right this wrong and if he did return, I knew he could do it. They'd celebrate his return to civilisation in the streets and he'd become the official President within days. Then, once he held the so-called highest seat in the land, he could finally break free from the control of his father, relying on the belief that his own parent wouldn't hurt him. But I knew that wasn't true. Parents were more than capable of hurting their children. More than capable of wanting to kill them. I dreaded the day I confronted my mother about Leo. I knew that one of us wouldn't walk away from the interaction and I couldn't place my bets on which one of us it would be.

the Téssera had built over the last several decades. His dad would always choose his ideals over his child, just like my mother.

the Téssera had built over the last several decades. His dad would always choose his ideals over his child, just like my mother.

morning walk around the safe house. It wasn't much freedom but after ten laps I felt like my blood was flowing and my mind was settled. It was an important part of my routine to keep my sanity, and I was determined to keep it this time around. I would stay logical. I repeat this mantra to myself as my feet fall into a predictable pattern and my body leaves them on autopilot.

If I lost control again like I had at the wedding, or at Rus's execution then the Settlement had no hope for a cure. I didn't feel guilt over Paul's death the way I had the man in grey. True, they had both been monstrous men cut from the same cloth, but Paul's death had felt righteous. The world had needed me to right his wrongs. The man in grey's murder had been a spur-of-the-moment rash decision I was only just beginning to forget. Paul's murder had been poetic. Then again, murderers always claim the first kill is the hardest. That's what I was now, wasn't I? A murderer. One death short of a serial killer.

If I were to meet Jack again would I let him live? Would I be able to carry on knowing I'd let him walk free when he was another wrong to be righted? He would never face legal ramifications for Leo's murder. Even if we pulled some form of evidence together, and believe me, Georgia was trying, the State would never listen to us. The narrative of a Dweller murdering my husband was more fitting to their political agenda. And even if, somehow, the State did support re-opening the my morals for so long

The sunflower was unusual. I hadn't noticed it before. The ground it was planted into was freshly dug. I gave the stem a small tug and the roots easily let go of the soil that held them. I apologised to the flower and placed it back in the grass, mud catching under my nails as I replanted it. Sunflowers weren't a native plant to our earth, someone must have taken care to plant it here and I'd ripped it from its bed callously. I couldn't help myself though, the large bright flower stirred up fond memories I'd rather forget. Mum had always had a vase of sunflowers in our kitchen at our family home. To begin with, I figured Dad brought them for her but after he left, they turned up every Monday without fail at our door. They were her favourites, a love passed down to her from her birth mother. She'd tell me about her biological mum, my grandma, sometimes. But more often than not it was too painful for her to remember those she'd left behind on Earth One. Something even at a young age I could sympathise with.

She'd tell me that the flowers would make her smile every time she looked at them, how the strong and thick stalks that held the bright heads reminded her that a thing can be strong and beautiful. It didn't have to be one or the other. Occasionally she'd call me her sunflower. The memory of my mother's love for me caused a wave of warmth across my heart that I didn't want. That woman had ordered the death of my husband. Had risked my son's life. She'd taken so much from me. I wouldn't love her any more. I couldn't.

morning exercise short and burst through the door of the safe house. Ryle and Georgia were engaged in gentle conversation over their coffee mugs and a third was lying in wait ready for me. They both turned to look at me, confused as to why I had entered the house with such passion.

"We have to leave."

There isn't time for explanations or arguments, so I move past them towards my room, ready to pack my bag and flee. But things were never straightforward with these two, they always wanted answers. I sighed loudly as Georgia followed me into my bedroom. "You really need to pack." It's been two years since Violet died in my arms but I still felt the need to keep my words at a minimum. They weren't worth as much to me without her around to hear them.

"What's happened?" Georgia returned my tone. I knew the grey cloud that had hung over me since that day was grating on her, I knew I was difficult to live with but I lacked empathy. She'd cared for Violet too I know, but she'd never loved her. Not like I had. I'd lost the two biggest parts of my heart over the last three years and now all that remained was a husk of my former soul. If I had at least been allowed contact with Franklin perhaps that would have kept the embers of my humanity smouldering but no, it was too dangerous. I wouldn't put my love and need for my child above his life.

"Di knows where we are."

mother's base, a way to avenge Leo's memory. Ryle had stopped that plan immediately. It was better to take our time, concentrate on the cure and work our way back into society. Once we had the public back on our side then it would be easier to retaliate for the crimes she had committed against me.

Georgia doesn't press me anymore, she doesn't ask me why I'm so certain that our location is no longer safe. She knows me well enough to know that I'd only demand this of them if I was certain, we were after all working our way back towards the safe house nearest the Dweller lab. I wouldn't put our route in jeopardy unless something serious had happened. She walks out of my room, leaving the door to slam behind her and I take a breath to steady myself as I pull my backpack closed. Three pairs of jogging bottoms, six T-shirts, ten pairs of underwear, and the same in socks. I never unpacked fully for the week we settled in each house, the only thing I ever removed from my pack without fail was my laptop and notebook. When I thought back to my wardrobe full of outfits in my marital home my heart constricted. A full rail of options that allowed me to display my chosen personality for the day. God, I miss my old life. It had been so simple and I'd never realised it.

Now wasn't the time for a walk down memory lane or to long for the material possessions I could never admit to missing. Now was the time for action. We had to run.

central zone, his rotten fingers yanking my hair from its roots as he did so. Some nights I could smell the putrid breath from his decomposing lungs as his body crushed me in my bed, leaving me powerless to run or call for help. His flesh slipped from his face in sizeable chunks as he screamed obscenities at me for ruining his grand scheme. I felt no guilt over his death. He was nothing more than a figment of my fear. If the State captured us then they would execute us all. I would lose the two people I had left on my side. The Settlement would lose any hope of a cure. Franklin would lose his mother. I couldn't let that happen. That's what I focused on when Paul haunted my dreams. I focused on survival.

I walked into the living room and placed my pack on the kitchen table. Georgia was the first to emerge from her room, pack thrown over one shoulder. I watched as she moved towards the knife block, considering each blade before placing her hands on the sharpest. She wrapped it in a tea towel and placed it into her bag. She shook her head at me, urging me not to tell Ryle she was armed. He didn't agree with us preparing for battle, and said it was a bad omen. Initially, Georgia had ignored this request, making sure to always carry something she could use as a weapon on her person. She stopped after about eighteen months. She finally accepted we were safe without having to spill any blood.

Ryle joined us, picked up his mug, and finished his coffee. I could murder this man. He was infuriating. Was he taking his time to prove a point?

hardly something I could schedule into our plans.

"We need to get out of this house."

Georgia had my back; she might not understand the reason for my fear but she knew me well enough to know it was true. Ryle fidgeted with his backpack and that's when I realised the reason for his delay. He didn't have a plan. We didn't have an escape plan.

"Out of the house. Now."

I issued the order and walked out of the front door, hoping that they would follow. If nobody else was going to get us out of danger then that responsibility would have to fall upon my shoulders.

I looked around outside the house, trying to find somewhere we could hide. A smattering of trees about five hundred yards away would have to do. I had no doubt that Ryle had made a call to Bailey. The cogs would already be turning in her mind, working out a way to extract us from this situation without harm. I just had to keep us alive long enough for that to happen.

I could hear Georgia and Ryle's footsteps following behind me as I walked wordlessly toward the trees. I can't deny my disappointment in Ryle, he was still just a pawn in someone else's grand scheme. I hoped for better from him after all we'd been through, after all I'd forgiven. If he'd had his way we'd still be sat in the kitchen finishing our coffees waiting for someone to ride in and rescue us.

It was obvious from the look on Georgia's face that she felt the same. There were many times over the last two years that I could tell she struggled with bowing to friendly words, that I wasn't sure I knew how to anymore. It's not that I was unfriendly, I was just distant. It was safer to be distant. I couldn't lose anyone else I cared about so the easiest solution was to stop caring. Or at least stop letting the universe see that I cared. Maybe then it would give me a break and stop the cruelty it insisted on inflicting on those I was close to. Leo. Regina. Violet. How many more people had to die before it was done with me?

I blinked slowly and took a breath. I couldn't let my mind spiral like this, I had to stay sharp and focused if we wanted to survive.

Focus on something you can see. The trees.

Focus on something you can smell. Dampness.

Focus on something you can touch. The ground.

Focus on something you can hear. Footsteps.

A lot of footsteps. Brash footsteps heading towards the safe house.

The kind of footsteps that want you to know they're coming because there is nothing you can do about it.

The kind of footsteps that carry death upon their backs.

eyes, I ducked down into the bushes that were overflowing at the roots of the trees. Ryle and Georgia followed suit. Wordlessly we all shrank as far back into ourselves as possible; the suns were still rising and we were relying on the cloak of dawn to keep us hidden. If we were still here when day finally peaked its head over the horizon we would be spotted for sure. It felt as though my heart was trying to beat itself out of my chest to escape. We'd spent so long running that I'd forgotten how terrifying the threat awaiting us was. I'd grown accustomed to thinking of it as something that would never happen. We all grew too complacent with our safety and now reality was surrounding our safe house.

Georgia reached for my hand as she heard my breathing increase in speed. Human contact was foreign to me now but I didn't pull away. I needed my friend to keep me grounded. If I had an anxiety attack like I had at Franklin's birthday party then we'd be spotted for sure. Thrown to the braying mob still out for our blood after all this time. I can't say I blame the people of the Settlement for their anger, it was just misdirected.

I watched Georgia's face out of the corner of my eye, it had softened into a smile somewhat. She gave my hand a squeeze and I realised I was the source of her small happiness in this moment. She'd missed me. I had been by her side for every hour of the last 730 days and she'd missed me for each of them. She missed her friend. A small wave of guilt washed over me as I remembered every time she'd tried to connect with me knew exists anymore?

The Paige she'd first met all those years ago in the hospital would never have sunk to the levels I had. That Paige had sworn to protect life at all costs. That woman was still fighting against her mother's instincts. That woman was dead.

I was my mother's daughter now, through and through. My hands were covered in the blood of those I felt had wronged me and I now operated alone. Di would be proud I'd cut emotional ties with those around me. Emotions make you weak she used to tell me when I'd come home from school crying about something one of my friends had said to me.

They make you weak my darling and you aren't weak.
Let them say what they say and do what you have to do.

Even when I was young I fought against her teachings, going back to school the next day and apologising to the friend who felt I'd wronged them enough to spit venom at me. I was a people pleaser. I'd thought back then that if people loved me and cared about me they would keep me safe. In a way, I hadn't been wrong. Ryle and Georgia cared about me, that's why they were still by my side. Violet cared about me and that's why I'm standing here today. If she never came for me in the corridor I would have been captured by security. She saved my life. So yes, having the love of people protects you. But I hadn't been able to protect those I loved. Those I still love.

We watched as the owners of the footsteps finally made themselves visible. They were human but it was the sunflower so early, I was obviously supposed to spot it as I was dragged from the safe house and taken back to her sanctuary. A way for her to say "gotcha," to let me know that somewhere she was smiling. To let me know she had won.

My mind began to worry about Franklin. Was he currently in a similar situation? Was the home he shared with Rus surrounded by strangers under my mother's bidding? Would Rus and Theo fight for him? There was no way Mum would only come for me tonight. She'd want to reunite the whole family and keep us under her powerful thumb. A part of me longed to step out of the clearing and hand myself over to the mob. At least if I was trapped in my mother's sanctuary I could finally be reunited with my child. Losing my freedom wasn't an enormous sacrifice when you compared it to the joy it could bring.

As though she could read my mind Georgia pulled on my hand, a way to tell me not to do anything rash. Not to do anything stupid. Ryle was now knelt down at the other side of me, making a point of not allowing any part of our bodies to touch but I could feel the warmth and fear emulating from him.

"What should we-" he tried to whisper to me but I raised a single finger on the hand closest to him. Now was not the time for words. Not with the enemy so close. All it would take was one gust of wind in the wrong direction and we'd be done for.

I watched in fascination as the group of strangers stood like statues around the safe house. Nobody the enemy in front of us was not to be underestimated, they were too dangerous for us to make a mistake.

Ryle went to speak again. That man never ran out of words but fell silent as we watched the figures move in unison around the house, each with their own can. The smell of petrol wafted through the air all the way to my nostrils in the clearing and I had to fight back a sneeze. They were setting up the threat to drive us out from the house, not realising we were already on the move away from them. I waited for one of them to talk, to call out to us and explain the peril we were facing. They'd expect us to come marching out, heads hung in shame at finally having been caught. We'd been faster than them though, smarter. How long would they wait for a response that would never come? Would it be long enough for us to put some extra distance between us?

I wasn't keen on waiting around to see what their reaction would be when they realised we weren't home and so I slowly stood as far up as I dared and took a few tentative steps backwards, keeping my eyes constantly focused on the enemy in front of us. Ready in case we were spotted. Ryle and Georgia followed suit, the three of us walking backwards until we were further into the forest and it was now difficult to make out the distinguishing features of the figures around the safe house. That's when the fire started. I thought it strange that they hadn't called out to us yet, hadn't revealed the threat of death they had around the building but my need to survive had overwhelmed my curiosity and now

Ryle's father, the man who had spent a lifetime grooming his only son to become President. Killing Ryle would anger the Settlement in a way they couldn't predict and wouldn't be able to contain. It made no sense. None of it made any sense.

We were far enough away from the house that I felt confident enough to take my eyes off the now-burning building. It was time to run. It wouldn't take them long to notice the lack of screams from within the inferno and then they'd expand the search. We only had a small window of opportunity within which to disappear. Ryle and Georgia were running at my side, we no longer cared about the crack of twigs beneath our feet confident that the roar of the flames would cover the noise.

They would have realised we'd escaped by now and the sound of their footsteps would soon take over the landscape around us if we didn't keep running. My feet already ached but I knew I couldn't give in to the instinct to rest just yet.. I was struggling to get my bearings on where we were. The forest looked the same as all the others we travelled through. There were no monuments I could use to pinpoint our location, nowhere safe we could aim to reach. We were lost. Despair washed over me causing my steps to falter and I nearly tripped over my foot. Luckily Georgia noticed the shift in my body's weight and reached out a hand to steady me.

"Be careful," she warned before picking up her pace again. I shook off the nerves that were descending

I can't believe the words have left my mouth and yet I know they are true. They were hunting us as a group, as individuals it would be harder to track us down. They would need three sets of eyes upon us at all times rather than one. Ryle and Georgia both stop running and spin around to look at me, anger at my suggestion radiating from them.

"Absolutely not!" Ryle raises his voice before Georgia can agree.

"Keep your voice down!" He's forgotten that we're in danger right now and I need to remind him. He let his emotions cloud his logic.

"We need to stay together. We've always been together." Georgia steps towards me as though she believes this is fear talking, as though she believes maybe finally the stress of our situation has broken my resolve.

"We're safer apart."

"We just need to keep running. Bailey will find us."

He had so much hope in his aunt that I nearly wanted to agree with him just to keep that alive. But the truth was Bailey probably had about as much clue where we were right now as we did. There were no spies out here keeping tabs on our whereabouts. We were alone.

"How can she find us when we don't know where we are? Ryle, trust me. We have to split up."

He has to believe me. He's the more malleable one out of the two of them. If I can get him on side it will mean Georgia is outnumbered. It will mean that I will have won and they will be safe.

does. I ensured my child was safe and loved. Now I had to do the same for the two people who had given up everything to help me find a cure.

"If we split up we will be harder to trace." A truth. "We'll be safer. All of us." A lie. "Please, you know it makes sense." Believe me. Believe all of my words.

Ryle hesitates in his defiance. I've won him over. "Maybe," he murmurs as he thinks through my suggestion.

"We can all meet back up at a certain spot and a certain time. Once they've lost our scent." I keep my words tight, knowing that the agent still lurking inside Georgia appreciates efficient communication.

"Where?" She asks which surprises me. I was expecting Ryle to agree to my plan first but no, she's the first one to understand my logic.

"We'll meet at the lake by the Waterfall. In two weeks' time." The restaurant I'd been supposed to have my anniversary meal in. The reservation we never made.

"Two weeks?"

Ryle is incandescent at my suggestion and he's not wrong. Fourteen days is a very long time when you're on the run and my idea of meeting back inside the Settlement, albeit under the cover of Nomad's land, was beyond dangerous. It would mean walking back into the lion's den.

"It's the last place they'd think to look for us." Georgia has puzzled it out and agrees with my reasoning.

out of his hands. If he wanted to be in charge, he should have planned for this, he should have been prepared for us to be discovered. But he hadn't planned for every possibility and now it had cost him his leadership. He was no longer in control of keeping us safe. That would be left to each of us.

The footsteps were approaching us now. We spent too long discussing our plan and now there was no more time.

"Go." I whisper to them, painfully aware of the slow march of death approaching us. They stand like rabbits in headlights and stare at me.

"Go. It will be okay," I promise.

Most likely a lie but even I'm not sure at this point about which words I mean and which I don't.

Georgia takes a step forward and squeezes my hand before she runs off to the left of us, further into the forest. Ryle hesitates for a moment longer. I can tell he wants to say something to me, he wants me to absolve him of all we've been through together. Perhaps of the lies he once told me. But now isn't the time for apologies and forgiveness, now is the time to act. I nod my head to the right of me and wait for him to move. He starts off slowly but eventually, I see his legs pick up their pace and soon he is gone. I turn around, facing the footsteps, ready to make my grand sacrifice. I wonder if Ryle or Georgia will return to this spot when they hear my screams, I hope not.

cover most of my face and I struggled to keep myself upright because of my lack of clear vision. I could feel the battle scars on the palm against my face and I knew with certainty that a Dweller was the one dragging me backwards. Had they been working in sync with the humans that had attacked the safe house? Was it all a ruse to draw us out into the open where we could be picked off one by one? It would explain why the attackers never tried to lure us from the safe house with threats.

I tried to dig my heels in, to at least make it more of a struggle to drag me away but in response, the Dweller merely picked me up around the waist with their other free hand and continued walking backwards further into the undergrowth. There was no point in screaming and I decided I wouldn't give them the satisfaction of my fear as they dragged me to my death. I would deny them that pleasure.

Without warning, I was forced down onto the ground in a kneeling position. The hand that had been lifting me from my waist was now in the small of my back ensuring that I would maintain my position. It was clear I had been placed in an execution stance, I readied myself mentally for the firing squad. Desperately, I tried to hide the fear and devastation that swirled inside my mind. We all fear our own mortality when the end seems near, I just didn't want to share that fear with my assassin.

hands on me right now. I'd be on my way to the Central Zone to await my punishment. Instead, I was hidden from their viewpoint, their victory stolen away from them by their sworn enemy. If I'd been able to move my face enough to smile at the irony, I would have.

In a way, I was glad it was the Dwellers that had won. I was glad they were the ones to capture me and that they would be the ones to end my life. At least they wouldn't take quite as much enjoyment out of my torture as the humans would. They weren't that cruel. They'd at least respect my life as they took it from this world. I wondered if they'd grant me one last request if they'd let me catch sight of Franklin before my execution. Of course, I didn't want to meet with him, not knowing that I'd be snatched from him so quickly, but just to set my eyes upon him one last time would mean I could leave this planet satisfied.

"You are a very stupid woman" whispered a voice I recognised. The Dweller's breath was hot on my ear as he delivered this line with a hint of compassion towards me. "If I uncover your mouth do you promise not to scream?" I nod as best I can and slowly the hand is peeled from my face.

I give thought to instantly taking back my word, to self-sabotage once again but the fact that this Dweller is a friend stops me. Elijio is kneeling behind me, his hand still in the small of my back to prevent me from jumping up and alerting the humans to our presence.

"We will give it a minute and then we will run."

me, but those scars were a reminder of the time he served on the front line and he was proud to display his loyalty to his people. Unlike Kyan, his jet-black hair was short, with the sides shaved into a central point at the nape of his neck. His facial features overall were softer than Kyans but his features were still unmistakably those of a Dweller.

His eyes were tilted up towards the bridge of his nose, which was thick and central. His lips were permanently parted thanks to an additional three tubercles within them. It left him looking as though he always had some wise words to impart. And he did to be fair to him. He was a very intelligent being and I had a lot of respect for him. But that didn't stop me from bristling at the fact he dragged me away from doing what I felt was right. If Ryle and Georgia came to any harm because I couldn't create a distraction, I'd do my very best to at least land a punch that would hurt, however unlikely I knew it would be that I'd even be able to connect my fist to his flesh before he reacted.

Dwellers had reflexes beyond anything humans had ever encountered, on this earth and the one before. It was almost as if they could move through time when needed. Not the most scientific explanation but the one that children liked to share on the playground and it has stuck with me. There was something magical about them, about all the unknown, unexplainable elements of them. Even before Mum had met Kyan I'd been intrigued by their kind. The God-like creatures walking amongst us.

He took my hand and pulled me to my feet. I knew it would have been quicker for him to carry me to safety but I respected he let me make my way there on my own two feet. He knew I was a proud woman.

We didn't speak as he led me through the forest that was slowly becoming less overgrown. As much as he felt confident enough that the noises of our feet would be covered by the surrounding calls of nature as it awoke, he was certain that our voices would carry to those who were hunting me. To be honest the silence suited me. It let me remind myself that logic would be the answer to this situation. I'd been emotional when I'd tried to sacrifice myself for my friends. Emotions made me weak, they made me act without thinking, and they made me into my mother. Not that she'd ever sacrifice herself. She was worth more to the movement alive than dead, after all.

Logically the solution to this situation was the cure. If I created the cure then I could prove to the Settlement that we weren't terrorists out for their blood. I could prove to the Dwellers that I had no vested interest in the disease, that there was no reason for my husband to have created it willingly. Yes. The cure was the answer and now I had Elijio by my side I was more certain than ever that I could find it. With the advanced technology he had access to at his lab, we could probably solve the problem in a matter of weeks.

My hand instinctively moved to my backpack, feeling for the reassuring bulk of my laptop. All my research and work so far was contained on it, not that considered a traitor, he would be shunned by the community and left to die alone. But he took that chance because the risk of us having no sample to work from was greater. He understood what I needed to achieve and had taken a gamble with his own safety in order to make sure that I did.

Violet would like Elijio. I could picture them working in the lab together, stolen whispers between them as they compared theories, glances they thought I'd miss as I took us down the winding path to the answer, and smiles shared over cups of coffee.

Did Dwellers drink coffee?

It didn't matter because in the comfort of my imagination, Elijio did and Violet knew exactly how he liked to drink it. God, I missed her. Every day I was reminded of her and would retreat into this fantasy land where she was still at my side. Still pushing me to achieve impossible tasks. The two of us would work together in our hospital lab for the day and then go back to my home, my actual home, where Leo would wait with dinner ordered and wine opened.

Every single night I fell asleep clinging to that daydream, longing for it to embed itself in my psyche ready for my REM cycle. I wanted to spend every sleeping moment with the two of them happy, truly happy back in their company. There was still a childish part of my mind that told me that this was nothing more than a nightmare, that soon I would wake up to the sound of Franklin's hungry protests over the monitor. Leo would roll over lazily towards me, flinging

Knowing in my heart that reality was as it was and my dreams were nothing more than fantasies was more torturous than nights upon nights of broken sleep. Every morning when the suns rose and I had to start another day without the three of them was just a crushing reminder of all I'd lost. All that had been robbed from me. I'd given up on being angry at Leo for working with the State long ago. I knew he hadn't really had a choice all along but it was easier to blame the dead than try to get justice from the living. The State was the real maker of this empty life I now lived. The State and my mother. If they'd all just left us alone, left us to live, then none of this would have happened.

By now we had been walking for nearly an hour in silence and the forest was growing thicker. It was getting more difficult to see the ground beneath my feet. Elijio sensed my trepidation and slowed his pace, falling into line with mine as he wordlessly guided me through the twisting roots that seemed to grab my ankles at every turn. By now I'd figured out where we were heading, or rather where we were. The sound of the animals around reminded me of my childhood when I used to crane my head out of the open window to try and pick up on their exotic calls. We were in Dweller territory.

My pulse remained steady despite this knowledge. I knew the Dwellers would find it easier to hunt me down here but I also knew they would be slightly kinder in their execution. If you know you have to die then you might as well look for the kindest option.

ones I have lost. Violet. Regina. Leo. Their deaths
would not be in vain if I could right the State's wrong.
      "As I said, for someone with as many brains in
your head, you are a very stupid woman."
I enjoyed the way Elijio talked, he'd confessed to me
that he'd never paid too much attention in his language
class and as a result sometimes he missed the occasional
word. It was endearing and refreshing. Which was a
good thing because I had a feeling that his voice would
be the only one I heard for a while.

of us each fending for ourselves seemed ridiculous to me, but I know when I'm outnumbered in an argument.

My plan had been to run out of sight and then return to the clearing and try to track one of them. It wouldn't have been difficult. My aunt had taken me out to the forest many times in my childhood and played hide and seek with me. She'd leave me facing a tree, with my face covered, and then hide nearby. Sometimes she'd blindfold me so I had to learn to rely on my hearing, but more often than not she would leave me a trail of subtle clues to follow. Looking back now it was a survival game dressed up as quality time but I still cherished the memories.

If I could track down one of them then we could protect each other. Not that Paige or Georgia truly needed my protection but it was an instinctual thought. We'd been safe together for so long, staying together had to be the better option.

I can hear the footsteps of the humans hunting us approaching. The fact they are still moving brings me comfort though, it means they have found no prey yet. For a moment I think about yelling out to them, calling them over towards me to buy my companions more time to escape but logically that would only confirm their locations to be near mine.

It would highlight that the three of us had been near, if not in, the clearing we had all run from. No. I needed to keep running and then keep my head down for two weeks until we could all reconvene. Perhaps can see the pain and guilt she keeps wrapped around herself. And we're unable to help her.

One day I hope that will change. I care about Paige, I truly do. I hated keeping the truth about her mother and the plans for my Presidency from her. But Bailey had warned me she was an emotional live wire and if she knew these truths it would jeopardise their escape plan. Because of course, we knew about their escape plan all along. We knew the moment they began discussing it with Lizzie. She was our spy inside the Anarchists, a way for my aunt to keep an eye on Di from afar.

The three of them were supposed to be safe and happy now. Reunited with their loved ones somewhere the State couldn't touch them. That was supposed to be my wedding gift to Paige - for her to finally be reunited with her son.

I was never a part of the escape plan; comfortable enough that being President in waiting would prevent any scrutiny or punishment from blowing my way. You can say a lot of things about my father but he always protected his interests. That had all fallen apart though the moment Paul and I had stepped into the corridor and spotted Violet and Paige. I knew exactly what would have happened if he radioed this observation to the team working for the Téssera that day, and I couldn't let that happen. I couldn't let them ruin the plan we all had been working so hard on. So I did what I had to do. I'd never intended for the man to die

up diving into the van and escaping alongside the three
of them. Well. Two of them in the end I suppose. Violet
never got the chance to feel free again.

My aunt had thought about that risk though.
Which is why she had the network of safe houses ready
to go. The driver had informed me of the change in plan
when we'd stepped out of the van to deliver Violet's
body. Bailey was prepared for everything. Paige would
probably tell me that meant she had a good chance of
being involved in everything but I knew that wasn't true.

Bailey was the closest thing to a mother I ever had.
She was the true parent who raised me and I knew her
better than she realised. All the years she had spent
nurturing and watching over me I had been watching
over her too. I knew Auntie Bailey like the back of my
hand which is why I was surprised she had no plan in
place for our current situation.

That's why I'd been so calm when Paige had first
explained that we needed to flee. I was certain that
Bailey would arrive at any minute to tell us what we
needed to do next. But she hadn't. Even when we'd
been stood watching them pour petrol over the safe
house I kept an eye out for her. I fully expected her
shadow to appear at my side at any minute with a fail-
safe plan to keep my friends safe. But she didn't appear.
For the first time in my life, my Aunt hadn't arrived to
save the day and I didn't want to think about the
reasons behind it.

I decided as I ran from the footsteps, that was how
I was going to spend the next fortnight. I was going to

whilst we'd been on the run. She only ever wanted to see me. She only ever trusted me. She always had a cloud of doubt around Paige, worried she was too much like her mother. And as for Georgia, she was a former employee of the State. Bailey was adamant, despite my protests, that no one can completely overthrow that level of brainwashing. No. I was the only one she could trust. I was family. And I trusted her implicitly as well. She'd always put me first throughout my whole life and I knew that would never change.

By now there was a general cramping beginning to emerge in my stomach and I knew a stitch was imminent. I had no choice but to slow my pace, massaging my abdomen as I did. I'd never been a big runner, even when I used to work out after particularly aggravating meetings with my father. I had always preferred boxing to cardio to stay fit and let off steam and over the last two years, I hadn't exactly performed any kind of proper exercise. I shouldn't have been surprised at my body's reaction to the high-intensity sprint I'd undertaken to save my life.

Easing my run into a brisk walk I kept my hand on my stomach as I took in my surroundings. I could hear the gentle hum of electricity that let me know I was near the border of Nomads land that connected with the main Settlement.

Not the wisest place for me to be, but I was confident enough in my drastic change of appearance. As long as nobody looked at me for too long, I would pass as another stranger in their day. I just had to be as

"I think you have me confused."

I put every ounce of seduction into my words as I turned around with a warm smile on my face. I truly was a politician, whether or not I wanted to admit it. You don't grow up with a father like mine and not learn a thing or two about how to talk to women.

She laughed as she took a step towards me and my cheeks flushed. I needn't have wasted my charm - it was only Carla.

"Nice to see a flash of the old Mayor is still in there."

I chuckled with self-depreciation. It had been a while since I'd had to put my best foot forward and it felt comfortable to slip back into it. Even if only for a moment.

"And it's nice to see such a friendly face."

It's her turn to blush now. It's a pleasant sight to behold. Carla is a very pretty woman, a fact that had not escaped my and Georgia's attention. I knew how dedicated she was to her husband, but a bit of gentle flirtation always helped the long evening walks between safe houses pass a little quicker. Once or twice I'd felt a twinge of guilt at flirting so openly with her in front of Paige. She was after all my wife but she'd clarified that since lying to her we were barely friends anymore. It was a shame because we had been growing close. Perhaps with time, we would have grown closer but now who knows. Perhaps we are both too damaged by our pasts to ever truly accept happiness into our lives.

"I think we ought to have a chat"

found her with me? I shuddered as I pushed the thought away. If that were to happen I'd explain that she was a quick fling on my way back to civilisation and send her away. She deserved to return home to her husband after all she'd risked for us.

Part of me hoped that wherever she was leading me would also contain Paige and Georgia. I knew the chances were slim to none but I still had a glimmer of hope in my heart. If Carla had found me then surely she may have also found my friends. Perhaps they were already waiting for me in a new safe house.

Once again I thought about how ridiculous the idea of splitting up had been. There was always safety in numbers, no matter what they said to oppose it. I wanted to be back with the two of them. It felt unnatural to be apart after so much time living in each other's pockets.

I kept expecting to look to my side as we walked to see Georgia falling into step with me. Given that Paige had locked herself in a bubble of her grief the two of us had grown quite close over the last few years. We had very little choice in the matter, it was bond or go mad with loneliness. I'm glad we chose the former. Once or twice I'd refer to her as Agent Cherry in jest, she'd always bat me around the head when I did so. She was determined she'd left that life and persona behind the day she'd found out the State created the disease. She swore an oath as an agent to protect the people of the Settlement and it had left a bitter taste in her mouth that those at the top had little regard for those at the bottom.

she had no interest in connecting with us. I was so lost in my thoughts and my melancholy at being separated from my friends, I didn't notice Carla go into the house up ahead.

Uncharacteristically, she hadn't paused at the threshold waiting to lead me inside. I'd never known her to lack manners so I had to assume she had a reason for wanting to enter before me. My heart rate picked up as I worried about what might wait for me inside that house. What if it wasn't the joyful reunion I'd been hoping for? What if she was waiting inside, readying to tell me that Georgia had been captured or Paige killed? Suddenly I didn't want to follow Carla anymore. I wanted to turn left down a side street and disappear. I didn't want reality to hit me.

A familiar face peeped out between the curtains and gestured to me. Bailey was inside that house. My aunt wanted to speak to me. I had never refused her before and I wasn't about to start now. Cautiously I opened the door and walked inside. Before I had a chance to take in my surroundings though a pain cracked through my side. Falling to the floor in agony, I look up to see Carla standing over me with a candlestick, she grimaces and then hits me across the back with it. What the hell is happening?

"Avoid the face if you can."

Bailey's voice commands from the other room as she appears before me, rope in hand.

"Hands," she barks at me, kicking me onto my back.

achieve her aim, no matter the consequences. I never thought Bailey would need to look at me like that.

Of course, that's her plan. She needs me to be injured to back up the story that I was taken against my will. She wants me to go back home to my father.

"I'm not going home." I protest as Carla slaps me across the face.

"I'm so sorry," she apologises looking as though she may cry.

"It's the best way to keep your friends alive."

And with those words, I know she's speaking the truth. The best way to protect Paige and Georgia from the State is to lead the State. So I lay there quietly and took the beating.

shack. It had a roof for which I was grateful, but the walls had definitely seen better days and if I wasn't mistaken I could see holes in them that had been haphazardly boarded up. Elijio noticed my critical eye as we approached the door and tried to shoot me a comforting smile but it failed miserably. I may have grown used to living like a true Nomad for the last two years but at least each of the safe houses had basic creature comforts and little to no draughts. If this was to be my new home then I had a feeling I was in for a rude awakening.

"It is safe" he offered by way of explanation and really, what more could I ask for at this point? Safety was the only thing that mattered. That and access to the lab.

"When can we start work?" My favourite thing about Elijio was that he never considered me blunt. He never minded my tone or second-guessed my words. He took them at surface value which, when I spoke to him at least, was exactly what they meant. There was no need to play games with Elijio. I didn't need to win him over or keep him on my side because he was a man of science and logic and that was a bond that brought us together.

"Nightfall." He pushed the door open with a creak and we stepped inside. "I cannot stay, home is calling." I didn't realise I was to live in this shack on my own. I hadn't been on my own for so many years now that I wasn't sure I remembered how to live with my thoughts warmth of his touch as the door closed behind him and I was plunged into darkness. Logically I knew that to have lights blazing in this shack would only draw attention to me but I was still relieved when my hands reached out and found a torch on a shelf.

Turning it on, I used it to take in my surroundings. There were holes in the wall and roof just as I'd expected but for now, at least, the air outside was calm. I'd have at least until true nightfall before I had to worry about the nightly storms. Plenty of time for some makeshift DIY. There was a blanket and some pillows on the floor, they looked clean enough and in the room's corner was a small door - a bathroom. To the left of me by the front door was a small sink and a gas stove. I had everything I needed to survive until Elijio returned with food but I still couldn't quite believe that this was now what I had to call home.

Pulling on my long-forgotten survival skills, I picked my way across the floor to the blanket and tore at the most worn corner, this would have to do for covering the holes up. I may be colder with fewer blankets when it came time to sleep but waking up soaking wet would be far worse. In the cabinet of the bathroom was a roll of what looked like tape and so I used it to attach the blanket squares over each entryway for the weather. Once satisfied that I'd made my shack as waterproof as possible, I sat down on the pile of pillows and tried to centre my thoughts.

Ryle and Georgia must have escaped as well. Surely we'd have heard the celebration of our hunters had they for the work that lay ahead of us. I need my brain in top condition if we were to find a cure. Find the cure and find our freedom. Simple enough. I'd faced worse odds before.

I woke to the sound of thunder rolling in and I could sense the presence of another person in what I guess I could call my kitchen area. Sitting bolt upright I was relieved to see Elijio's frame creeping around. Like most Dwellers he could move with no sound and it was most unnerving to watch him put food and supplies away with no noise. It was like watching the TV on mute.

"Honey, you are home" I didn't need to speak to let him know I'd awoken, he'd probably heard the change in my breathing once I was conscious. He turned to me with a smile and held out a plate towards me. "Here, eat and then we work." I stood up and gratefully took the plate from him. I did not know what any of the food before me was but I received it gratefully. The flavours weren't like any other mix I'd tried, not even in my mother's so-called sanctuary, but I enjoyed them nonetheless. As I finished my portion my belly gave a rumble in protest at my empty plate which caused Elijio to chuckle. "My wife knew you would enjoy that. There is more for you later but for now, we move."

I was very aware of my scent after a day on the run but it didn't seem to bother him, so I brushed off my usual need for high levels of personal hygiene and followed him from the shack.

sounds I'd never heard. The leaves on the trees seemed to glow in the moon, changing colour with each lightning bolt that turned the sky purple above us. Creatures skittered across the path in front of us and at one point I had to bat a flying beast the size of a baseball away from my face. All the things I'd imagined as a child were here and then some. I longed to take our time as we picked through the undergrowth. I wanted to soak up the world I now found myself in but Elijio's pace did not slow to match mine.

"Bad storm tonight" He pointed out. I worried about the rain. It usually came alongside weather as violent as this and although I was sure Elijio would be okay, no matter the downpour, I wasn't sure he was aware of the human disposition to burn in its heated drops. "We will arrive before it rains"

So he knew about human biology. At least a little. "Why are you helping me Elijio?" I couldn't help but wonder, after all if he was caught he would be considered a traitor and thrown out from the tribe. His family line would be struck from the records as though they'd never existed and all his achievements would be unwritten. Kyan had told me that loyalty was the thing Dwellers both valued and punished the most. You should always be loyal to your tribe, no matter what.

"Humans have done many wrongs. I can at least help right this one." He didn't turn to look back at me as he spoke and I knew his eyes were busy darting around taking in our surroundings, alert to danger or the appearance of another. He wasn't oblivious to the risks we'd first arrived on Earth Two. They'd taught us how to survive in the unfamiliar landscape and helped us set up and improve the technology and items we'd brought with us. In fact, they'd help build our Settlement, something the State was keen to forget. If it hadn't been for their kindness and strength humanity would be nowhere near as advanced as it now was.

We'd arrived on Earth Two with industrial 3D printers and blueprints to every invention ever patented. The Dwellers had asked to borrow the plans and we'd shared them willing. When they returned they brought back not only the finished products themselves but also upgrades for them. Ways to streamline our productions and improve efficiencies.

Our factories relied on their technology to produce our food, our power and items like our cars. The furniture in our homes, the everyday items we all took for granted, all of that had been thanks to their advice and sympathy at our plight. Without the Dwellers our first settlers might never have survived let alone thrived. And yet we'd engaged them in a never-ending war, some gratitude that was.

Elijio pushed on ahead of me and I had to quicken my pace to keep up. He had no intention of answering my question, small talk wasn't something he had time for but I had to know what he meant.

"I'm sorry about the war." The words were so pathetic that it made my skin cringe. How could I hope to apologise for the actions of so many with just a few small words?

back of him, he turned round to look at me with an expression I couldn't read. Anger. Sadness. Resentment. "You do not know the words you speak."

"Look," I hold my hands up, palms facing him as a sign of peace, "I don't have any sides in this. I'm just saying you can't rewrite facts."

"And yet, you do." He turned away from me and continued walking down the path. I knew Elijio wouldn't harm me but I was still unnerved by his tone so I picked up my feet and followed him silently, no longer wishing to carry on this disagreement.

True to his word we arrived at the side door to the laboratory just as the rain began to fall from the darkening clouds above us. He didn't need to brief me on the protocol for entering the lab, we'd done it together so many times. Stay small, stay silent and stay in line. It wasn't much different to the way Paul had made me live for so many months, so it didn't feel foreign to me.

I followed him down the corridor, staying close to the wall so he could cover me with his frame should we bump into any of his colleagues. He relied on shadows to keep me under wraps as we moved towards his office. I liked Elijio's office. It was clean and well-organised, much like my own had been. It was like coming home after a long day and I felt the tension release from my shoulders. Being in this room meant we were one step closer to a solution. That I was one step closer to my son. As though he could read my mind and bounds ahead of what she expected from a human child. I hoped that this interaction, this stage in his life living under Dweller care, would help mould him into a well-rounded and kind individual. A staunch ally to those the State stood against. She had offered her services as a way to provide support to our endeavour. Knowing the joy regular updates on my child would bring me.

I'd asked Elijio recently what others thought of his wife's interactions with the humans and he just told me they paid the words of others no mind. They weren't breaking any laws nor being disloyal to the tribe, in fact, they were helping to support guests of the Helsas - a noble cause. I would never stop being grateful to Violet's ex, Tendai, for the protection he is offering my friends and my son. He is the only reason they are still alive.

I sat down at the smaller chair next to Elijio's desk and pulled out my laptop and notebook. It was time to get to work.

"Now is not the time for notes" he explained as he gestured towards a small side door I'd never been permitted to go through before, "now is the time for science."

seen before. The only thing I recognised was a compound microscope, though it had more bells and whistles than any I'd ever seen before. It was then that I realised that Elijio had never let me into his actual lab. Just the side office where he would provide me with reports on his findings whilst keeping the tech away from me. To be fair it wasn't a poor decision. I wouldn't know where to begin when it came to handling some of this gear. I imagined Violet standing beside me in this moment, a look of awe on her face as she took in the gadgets at our disposal. She'd love being here, a whole new world of possibilities lying before her. It still hurt to think about her, even after all this time, but I didn't fight the thoughts anymore. They kept her alive in some strange way, they kept her with me even after she was long gone.

"I have inputted all the previous data and the sample since you were last here. I worked on our latest hypothesis but unfortunately, it was a failure." He was as frustrated by our lack of progress as I was. We'd been so certain we'd cracked the code the last time we'd been here that it was deflating to realise we'd been wrong once again. I wasn't sure why he couldn't deliver that news to me earlier on in the day when he'd first let me into the shack, perhaps he very much kept his work strictly in the lab, unlike me.

My mind was always focused on the disease, always focused on the cure. My notebook was full of late-night scribbles and questions that I never got around to

"We need a sample."

"I've already given you the sample."

"No, Paige, we need a human sample." Of course we did. How had I not thought of this? We were trying to create a cure for humans with no human DNA to test it on. He needed samples from me.

Elijio saw the understanding on my face and moved towards a cabinet. He pulled out a handful of medical equipment and gestured for me to sit in a nearby chair. "This will only hurt a little." He wasn't wrong. The sensations as he scraped my skin, swabbed my nose and drew my blood barely tickled, not like when we did it back home. It was as though the instruments were numbing the areas as they went but leaving no trace of anaesthesia. I certainly didn't feel groggy once he had finished. Fascinating.

Taking the samples over to a computer I watched as my DNA threads appeared on the screen that took up the largest part of the wall. I'd never gotten over just how interesting the human body could be when it was reduced to parts and numbers and I hoped I never did. That was the driving force behind my work, why I chose the profession I did. There was no greater mystery than the human body. Built so well and yet so poorly. The organs that kept us alive could also kill us should something be out of sync.

Mum had never really understood that side of my brain, and despite his support, neither had Grandpa Joe. I didn't truly meet my people until I started my higher education and began working at the hospital. There I upon his face, his expression was as measured as ever. I felt a bit disappointed by this, perhaps Elijio and I weren't as similar as I'd first hoped. Maybe he didn't find the magic in science the same way I did.

"Now we can run the scenarios. I built them based on your last few hypotheses, I hope you do not mind." I shook my head although in truth I did mind. I didn't want a computer to outsmart me. I wanted to come up with the answer. I wanted to be the hero. I try to quieten my ego but now that truth, that desperate need to be the one who puts things right, has entered my mind I can't forget it. Am I only motivated by my need to be the saviour? Is that the only way I'll forgive myself for unleashing the disease upon the Settlement if I'm the one who spends hours after hours slaving away in a lab finding a way to save them all? Would that be enough?

As much as I knew it wasn't my fault we had crashed that day, that it had been a mixture of the State's and my mother's fault, it had been my hands on the steering wheel. My inability to drive had caused us to go flying into the lake. That had all been on me. Before I could wallow too deeply in blame and self-pity I turned my focus onto the computer screen, as numbers and letters I didn't recognise whizzed past my twirling DNA strains.

"What's it doing exactly?"

"Building and testing scenarios based on your notes and findings. Think of it as your second brain. Programmed to think the same way you do."

"Until it finds a solution. Could be a day, could be an hour, could be a year."

That didn't sound very promising. "Can I help it at all?"

"You can add your notes in over here, give it more of your thoughts and it will become more aligned to your process."

I walk back to the office and pick up my notebook. This was all so strange, the idea that a computer could be programmed to think scientifically as I do. If we had this back in the Settlement I could solve any project or ailment. I could have fifty of myself in one lab all working towards a common goal. The thought of multiple brains both excites me and fills me with dread. I could barely cope with my brain let alone several carbon copies of it. And would they grow to replace me? Could they? When I was dead and gone could they carry on my work on my behalf? Keep humanity healthy?

The possibilities were endless and I dreamt up different scenarios as I inputted my notes on the keyboard in front of me. Elijio had been kind enough to plug in a human keyboard for me so I at least recognised the letters and numbers as I typed them in. It was yellowed and some keys stuck down when pressed but it was certainly easier than having him translate it into his native tongue.

"We will need a study group once we have a possibility." I nod as I finish inputting the last of my thoughts into the computer. "They'll need to be human"

"How do we get the word out?"

"You do not. You stay quiet. I will get message through network and have them come to your home for testing."

The idea of conducting scientific tests on live subjects in what Elijio referred to as my home was less than ideal. It was hardly a sterile environment, but I guess we had no other option. We couldn't have a parade of humans traipsing through the corridors of the Dweller laboratory.

"Now we go home. The patrol will be here soon." We never spent more than a few hours in his lab at a time. Security guards would periodically check each office to make sure there were no moles lurking to steal Dwellers' secrets. No humans waiting with nefarious ideas.

As we're moving back towards his main office Elijio's ears prick up and his lips curl, something is wrong. Without words he places his hand on the small of my back and guides me toward a cupboard in the corner of his room, he opens the door silently and points inside. I don't have the Dweller ability to move without sound but I try to be as quiet as my clumsy human limbs allow me as I climb into the cupboard and let him close the door on me.

It's pitch black within these small walls but thankfully I don't suffer from claustrophobia. Leo did though. He even dreaded the elevators at the hospital despite the fact they were big enough for a gurney and six medical personnel. I'd always reach for his hand husband so I found it endearing that something as simple as close spaces could cause his adrenaline to peak. The horrors he saw every day in his job and the risks he took in his side work never caused even a bead of sweat to escape from a pore but he'd always leave the lift with a damp patch on his shirt just below his shoulder blades.

I was happy to let my memory wander to thoughts of Leo. Now I'd realised all of the truths behind our accident and his murder my brain would now allow me to look back on our time together with happiness rather than terror or guilt. I looked forward to the day that would happen to memories of Violet. For the time being whenever I tried to think of her, I came back from my walk down memory lane with tears threatening to spill. I still hadn't dealt with the horrors of her murder and so I wasn't allowed to indulge in tales of happier times gone by. I wasn't sure how I'd ever deal with it. It wasn't like with Leo where I could take justice into my own hands by attacking Jack. I could hardly wage war on the State-issued bullet that had ripped through her chest. I was just one woman, there was only so much I could do.

I took long and slow breaths as I stood in the cupboard's darkness, hyper-aware that Dwellers had sensitive hearing, and listened as Elijio sat down at his desk, intentionally scraping the chair backward as he did so. He was inviting whatever had unnerved him to find him, to hunt him, to show it he had no fear and nothing preferred science to battle which is why he spent his days in the lab rather than on the front line or hunting. Would he be able to defend himself against whatever was out there? Would he be able to defend me?

I decided at that moment, if I felt Elijio was in danger I would throw the cupboard door open and create a distraction. I would allow them to capture me if it meant he could escape. He had already done so much for me and my race that the least I could do for him was make sure he got home safely.

An unfamiliar voice appeared in the room on the other side of my hiding place, deep and powerful. The two of them exchanged words in a language I could never hope to understand. The irony of the fact they bothered to learn English, despite our ongoing war, and our schools didn't even teach a passing mention of their culture was not lost on me. The Dwellers had always welcomed us. They were still welcoming us in some small way despite our constant thirst for their blood and their land.

Elijio's voice was lighter than that of his guest and I strained my ears to try and picture their positions, but knowing they could move silently made this a fruitless activity. It wasn't until I heard the door slam behind them that I realised they'd both exited the office. Elijio must have let the door slam for my benefit. I hoped his companion hadn't noticed.

Not knowing whether or not it was safe for me to leave I decided to get comfy, sinking to the floor as best

head from my knees. How long had I been asleep? The cramp in my feet told me it had been a while and if I didn't want to make a mess in this cupboard I needed to find a restroom quickly. I tried to move my feet as quietly as I could but was unsuccessful and I rattled the doors. I paused whilst holding my breath waiting for someone to discover me but nobody came. I guess if there were any Dwellers nearby that they weren't on high alert and therefore hadn't dialled their hearing up. I took my chance and crawled out of the cupboard, sitting on Elijio's floor to stretch my legs out. The computer in his laboratory was beeping so loudly even my human ears could make the sound out. So why hadn't Elijio returned to check on our work?

As much as my curiosity wanted to investigate what the computer had found my need to take care of my bladder was more important. Now the feeling was returning to my toes I could finally stand and I took several soft steps towards the front door of his office. I knew the toilets were two doors down from this one but I'd never gone there unaccompanied. Who knew what I'd meet in the corridor and without Elijio's protection I would be a sitting duck. There was no other choice though so I pulled the door open a crack and peered outside, half expecting a pair of hands to reach in and grab me. But none came. The corridor was empty and this was the best chance I was going to get. I moved as quickly as I could towards the bathroom and felt instant relief as I made use of the cubicle.

with me sitting on a toilet seat terrified to move a muscle.

"Dr Hanson we know you are in there." The voice sounded softer than Elijio's but still held an air of menace about it. The prey instinct inside of me could sense the danger I was in. I looked around me, desperately wishing for a window to appear behind me I might be able to climb out of. I knew Dwellers could easily outrun me but if I had the chance, I at least had to try. I owed it to Franklin to try.

"There is no way out." The voice wasn't wrong, I hadn't managed to conjure an escape route through sheer force of will. I should have stayed with Ryle or Georgia. Why did I insist that we all had to go our own ways? At least if I'd stayed with them then there would be two of us against two of them right now.

"We will not kill you." The voice probably meant for this to bring me comfort but I couldn't help but pick up on the word we. They weren't going to kill but somebody else might.

The cubicle door shook lightly as they took their frustration out on it, a light tap as far as they were concerned but heavy enough to rock the hinges. I had no choice but to open the door and face whoever stood on the other side and so with every bit of courage I had available to me in that moment, I placed my hand on the lock. I slid it backward as slowly as I was able, my survivor instinct working against my logical mind. There would be a way out of this, it whispered to me, there would be a way to escape if I could just buy myself when I'd get upset.

Never let them see your weaknesses.

Standing in the bathroom in front of me was a human woman, about ten years my junior, and a Dweller who looked like a young Elijio right down to the adorned scars. The three of us stared at each other as the tension around us grew. I wondered for a moment if I could make it to the bathroom door before they did. After all I was closer so would have a head start.

I knew I could easily take care of the human if I had to. I could push her against the sink and let gravity take control as I had with Paul. But when it came to fighting the Dweller I knew there would be no hope of victory.

"Elijio sent us" the Dweller spoke without invitation, the first to break the silent stand-off. "You must come with us."

I didn't know whether or not to believe him and the feel of his grip on my arm as he led me towards the bathroom door told me that I didn't really have a choice. No further words were exchanged until we were out of the lab and walking down the path back towards my shack. It wasn't until then that the Dweller let go of my arm.

The human woman coughed lightly and I turned to look at her. She had mousy brown hair and green eyes. There were no special features upon her face to make her attractive. I could see as she fell into pace next to me, that her front teeth were crooked, she had three of turning round to look at us. Specimen?

"He means lab rat," she offered softly, no sense of sadness in her tone. Acceptance. She had accepted her lot in life.

"Test subject is the official term" I've instantly switched masks to Dr Paige Hanson, lead scientific researcher and this makes me able to switch off my empathy towards her. She seemed here of her own free will. The Dweller did not attempt to force her out of the lab and down this path as he had me. She was with him, they had come together to collect me. She must be aware of the risks and thankfully she would have plenty of time to think them over as we developed the cure ready for the test.

"Elijio sent this," the Dweller doesn't break from his pace so I have to jog to catch up with him to take a syringe from his hand, "it is a prototype" he offered by way of an explanation. Bored at having to interact with humans he picks up his pace so I could no longer keep step with him unless I began sprinting. By now I could see the outline of my shack in the clearing. How had Elijio developed this? Is that what the computer had been so eager to tell us about?

I wouldn't inject this woman with a compound I had no knowledge of. I couldn't do that. Even my scientific brain wouldn't allow me to switch off my empathy that much. Who knows what the ramifications would be for her? And I wouldn't know how to help her if it all went wrong without knowing what I had injected into her.

sentence trails off. She's fully aware of the risk she is about to undertake and is trying to save me from humanising her too much. If I humanise her then I won't be able to risk killing her. Every other clinical trial I've been involved in over my career has been controlled, methodical, and carefully overseen by trained medical professionals who could quickly undo most side effects my cures could cause in their early days.

The mortality rate from our trials was only 5% and we'd tested our experiments on hundreds of people over the years. I was proud of the work I'd done before, proud of the lives I'd saved, as well as the lives I'd protected during the trials. This would be different. This would be life or death for this woman and I was testing something I wasn't even aware of.

"I can't work under these circumstances" I turn to the Dweller, expecting him to cower under my defiance. It's the tone I'd used on the board members so many times before, full of pride and danger, a way to bend people to my bidding. Honed to perfection after years of studying the strong women around me. He barely even blinked as I spoke.

"Elijio says you must. Says it is the only way."

"I want to speak to him."

"It is impossible currently. He is still speaking with security. He will be back tomorrow."

"Then we wait."

"There is no time to wait. You trial cure now."

"No." I was through with other people controlling my life. My life hadn't been my own since the day of the arm, twisting it behind my back.

"Do not be stupid" he warns and I can feel the hate and resentment ebbing from him. Whoever this Dweller was, he was not a sympathiser. He was not on my side. He was on Elijio's side but not mine. He wanted to kill me, I could tell. It's animal instinct to know when you are in mortal danger, that instinct may come a second too late but it always comes in the end.

"It's okay" offered the woman, placing her hand on my free arm. The one that still held the syringe, "We have to do this." She sat at the chair by the table and rolled her sleeve up. "If you don't do it then I will, and I'll probably end up doing it wrong, hit an artery or something."

She smiles at me, trying to comfort my nerves in this moment. She should be the one in need of comfort, it's her life on the line. And yet here she is, trying to help a stranger, when potential death is just a syringe push away. This woman is too good a person to waste on an uncontrolled experiment. She deserves to be given the cure someplace safe and clean. She deserves better odds than those I can give her right now.

The Dweller releases his grip on my arm and I shake it out in annoyance. We exchange a glance and then I move towards the woman.

"Are you sure about this?" She nods once, her eyes firmly on mine.

"Do it."

I nod back and take the cap from the needle. Every medical instinct in my body is vibrating, trying to stop

blood seeps from her nose, her entire existence
disappearing before my eyes. Tears are pricking at the
corner of my eyes, she never stood a chance.

Before I can place a hand on her, to bring her
comfort as she moves from this life to the next, the
Dweller picks her up from the chair and slings her over
his shoulder like she's garbage to be disposed of.

"What was her name?" I ask with shaking breath,
trying to hold back the tears that are threatening to spill.
I won't let him see me cry. I won't give him the
satisfaction.

"I didn't care to ask." He responds as he leaves my
shack.

I have killed ten people since that first woman in my shack. Men and women of all races and ages. There was the woman with wild hair like my mother's, the older man who reminded me of Dr Raymond, and the young adult who made me think of Leo in his prime. So many faces had entered the shack and none of them had the chance to leave.

Elijio is kinder about it than his counterpart but each death still hurts. I don't think it's ever not going to hurt. Unlike with Paul, the man in grey or even my attempt on Jack's life, I never meant to kill those people. I meant no harm towards them. I was just doing my job. A job that Elijio insisted on.

When he finally showed his face in my adoptive home after the first death, I was vibrating with rage. As a doctor and a human with a conscience, I couldn't believe what he'd forced me to inflict on that woman. My brain was full of every hateful slur I'd heard about the Dwellers growing up. I had to bite the inside of my cheek to stop myself from spitting them at him. No matter how I felt, I couldn't allow that level of hate to seep onto my tongue.

He was calm and measured in his explanation if a little cold for my tastes. I'd often thought of my ability to extract myself from empathy for the better good of my work as unmatchable but Elijio made me pale in comparison. I didn't know if he would have felt the same had it been Dwellers' lives we were risking but I liked to hope so. I didn't want to think that he placed less importance on a life just because it was a human

He kept to his word and I was allowed to show my future victims some level of respect before inspecting them to find the cause of their demise. I then sent these findings with Elijio to the lab. I was no longer permitted to step foot in there after security nearly caught me last time, and he would return with a change in the compound. We were doing everything we could to make the cure less deadly and more effective but it just wouldn't work. After Elijio removed our eleventh victim from my shack, I drew a deep breath and spoke words I never thought I would as a scientific researcher.

"We need to stop."

"We have come too far to stop."

"I can't take any more lives."

"If you stop, the disease will take many more. You humans would take many more. How many need to die?"

"What does that even mean?" I know he believed the truth about the disease. That the State had created it to equal the playing field in the war against the Dwellers. But there was always something more beneath his words, some sad wisdom I wasn't privy to. A small form of resentment towards my kind that he'd never dared to speak aloud. "Why are you so sure that humans inflict death? We're not all like the State. We don't all revel in killing others."

"All of this started because of the State and it will end with the State if you don't take action."

A small smile pulls at my mouth at the rhyme in his speech but I feel no deeper joy. "It's not that poetic. They just want more land."

"They wanted more land on the treaty day." He's getting frustrated now. I can feel it seeping from his pours but I'm not afraid though he is nearly twice my size. Elijio is a kind person, he will not harm me. "They started the war."

"That's not true." My patience was wearing thin. I wanted to discuss stopping our trials for the cure and not fall into a history lesson. "You know that isn't true." He laughs gently at my naivety but it doesn't feel cruel or patronising. It never does with Elijio.

"You know what is true."

He's not wrong. It's what my mother always used to allude to when I still lived with her. I just never wanted it confirmed.

"We ambushed our own people, didn't we?"

A single nod from him confirms everything my mother had instilled in me when she used to protest against my State-sanctioned history lessons. I used to argue against her furiously, so sure that history was true and stable. So sure in my belief that her theories were just the webs of paranoia seeping through into our happy family life. But she was right. She'd always been right.

I don't know why it shocked me so much to have it confirmed by somebody else. I, more than anyone, knew first-hand the cruel lengths the State would go to to get what it wanted, but there had always been a part one." He sounded so sure of our success, despite the fact he'd promised me this on the last two batches and I'd still had to watch as someone sat across from me and died within minutes.

The last one had been a young man, well-spoken but full of resentment at the State for what they had done. He was one of the few in the Settlement who believed in my innocence. He'd lost his mother and sister in the first wave of the disease and wanted to do all he could to stop it happening to somebody else. I'd put all of my hope into the needle as I pricked his skin, willing the universe to let this man live. But he didn't.

None of them, so far, had continued to breathe after five minutes. Elijio saw the fact the time gap between injection and death was lengthening as a good sign, a way to be sure we were making improvements. I saw it as a form of torture, staring at the clock, counting down the minutes until their heart would stop beating.

I couldn't keep shutting off my humanity when I was the one with my finger on the needle. Of course, we'd always been sad when we lost one of the test subjects in the trials at the hospital but I was removed from the clinical trials. I didn't have to watch anyone die because my formula wasn't quite up to scratch.

"Can't somebody else run the trial?"

"You want to trust someone else?"

He was right. The only two people I knew I could trust and call upon were lost to me for another week, and that was if they made it to the waterfall safely to reconnect. I had no idea of their movements or

"No" I reply, knowing that this is the correct answer.

"New subject will be here soon."

As if on cue there's a knock at the door. Elijio opens it and a young boy, barely over eighteen, walks into my shack. He's accompanied by the unfriendly Dweller who had pulled me from the lab. He and Elijio speak in their native tongue before he passes a syringe across. They nod and then the resentful Dweller is gone. Elijio shakes his head to himself, clearly their conversation has not been a friendly one.

"You begin, if you excuse me." He hands me the syringe and motions for the boy to take a seat at the table before opening the door and following his friend outside.

I take my spot opposite him as I have done many times before and wordlessly he rolls up his sleeves. He's been briefed about the ban on small talk, as I remove the cap from the syringe. However, I can't help myself.

"Why are you here?"

He looks mildly annoyed by my question. "Got no place better to be" he smirks, wanting me to believe in his confidence.

"You know we've had no survivors yet." I'm not supposed to tell the test subjects this. I'm not supposed to let them know the odds we are facing.

"Someone has to be the first."

He's so young. He has his whole life ahead of him and yet he's willing to risk it all to help me find a cure. To help me stop the State.

me someone else, someone older, someone more aware of their mortality.

"Look, I just don't want to catch it okay?"

That was a first as far as I was aware. Somebody offering themselves up as a lab rat to avoid becoming infected.

"Why?"

"You know what that thing does to people? It changes them. Makes them into something different. So say I catch it and I can fly. And so I'm flying around here there and everywhere for a couple of weeks or even a couple of years because fuck it who knows. Right, and so I'm flying around being a hero on the State's dime and I save these two kids from the top tower of a burning building. And then it stops working. The infection has stopped and I can't fly anymore. And as I'm falling to the earth, looking at certain death, all I can hear is these two children screaming and crying about how they don't want to die or how they want their mummy and what am I supposed to say to them? Everything will be alright? Because they have eyes. They can see the pavement closing in. And I go to my grave with the sound of those children's screams, their breaking bodies, ringing in my ears? No thanks. That ain't a chance I'm willing to take."

He eyeballs me defiantly, daring me to argue against any of his points. I can't. Everything he is afraid of, is a fact.

His scenario was completely plausible. The disease changes human DNA in ways I'd never thought person in front of me was very aware of the risk he could face if he didn't at least try to stop it.

"You could wait and take the cure when it's ready though?" A last-ditch attempt to stop him, to stop me, although my needle is slowly heading for his flesh.

"Like I said Doc, that ain't a chance I'm willing to take."

We exchange a small nod and I push the plunger down into his arm, just as Elijio returns looking flustered. I don't know if he'd overheard our conversation but I assumed he was too wrapped up in his own to lend his attention elsewhere.

The boy and I stare at each other whilst Elijio stares at the clock. One minute. Two minutes. Three. Four. Five.

I wait for the tell-tale trickle of blood to start its river from the boy's nose but it doesn't come. He sits rigidly, breathing normally, never taking his eyes from mine. "Is that it?" He asks breaking the tension around us. Six minutes. Seven. Eight. Nine. Ten.

This is the longest we have ever had somebody live after injection but I can't celebrate yet. All we have proven is that the cure won't kill him. We haven't yet proven it will protect him from the disease or the mutations, we've only done that theoretically. But it's a step. It's a victorious first step towards the end of this madness.

"I will bring more food."

Despite him trying to hide it, I can see the twinkle of pride in Elijio's eyes.

He turns back to look at me accusingly, but there is sadness behind his anger. It's the one thing he was afraid of, the disease, and now he'd been told we'd intentionally infect him with it. His nightmare could still come true.

"We didn't know you would make it this far," explains Elijio. He rummages around in his pockets and pulls out a vial. With care, he places it in front of me. "This is a live sample, it will be infectious so be cautious. We will run the experiment when I return in the morning. It will give us enough time to be sure the cure hasn't killed you."

The boy doesn't turn to look at him as he leaves. Instead, all of his attention is focused on the glass vial in front of me. I can't lie. I felt a level of fear over it too. The liquid in this vial could kill us both or permanently alter our DNA and then kill us. Or it could give us the worst flu we'd ever suffered before leaving us to survive. That was the best-case scenario. That the disease itself wouldn't kill us or change us. That's what I was hoping for.

"My chip was green" he offers as he leans his head onto his arms and stares at the liquid closer. "Green means go" he chuckles sarcastically. "Dad was thrilled. Said I'd be able to serve the State and bring honour to the family. Mum was just happy it meant I wouldn't die. At least not straight away."

"I'm sorry" I can't offer him any words of wisdom, there are none at this moment.

My ribs still ached from the beating Bailey and Carla inflicted upon me and I bring my hand to cup the worse side, as I answer my father.

"The attack on the safe house was the perfect opportunity. They were so terrified of having been discovered that I could slip out into the forest and make my way back to the border."

He sat across from me in his armchair. He still lived in the same grand home I'd grown up in and the furniture, whilst regularly replaced, was never updated. The paint on the walls was fresh. I could smell it, but it was still the same shade of pale green my mother had picked out when they first wed. His refusal to move on from the past was the one thing I clung to when I considered my parents' relationship. He lived in the ghost of her decor because he'd truly loved her.

Unfortunately for her, just not more than he loved his position in society. I wondered if he ever regretted the decision to choose my life over hers. One day I hoped we'd reach the kind of relationship where I could ask him that. It was doubtful though that it would be a conversation he'd be eager to have. Perhaps it was more of a deathbed conversation.

"Is that the story you're sticking with?" He sounds unimpressed.

Probably because he's one of the few people who know it's all a lie. I have no doubt that he knows I worked alongside Bailey to try and free Paige from his control. He knows I went with them willingly and he more formal Father. He's always been Sir for as long as I can remember. I suppose when I was a toddler I was permitted to call him Dada, but as soon as I was willing to follow commands, he became Sir.

My aunt never used to refer to him as my dad either, she'd call him Anton, even when talking to me. I suppose it was a strange childhood in many respects but it didn't feel it at the time. I thought every child had to call their dad Sir and learn to recite the entire history of the Settlement on a whim. It wasn't until I turned eighteen and moved out that I realised that wasn't quite the case.

Still, the elocution lessons and years of finishing school made life a little easier for me when I finally achieved the freedom I'd longed for. People were drawn to me. I had an easygoing charm that I owed to my father and his plan for my future. And try as I might to find another career nothing suited me more than politics.

I told myself, after each election win, that this would be the one where I finally made a difference. Where I finally made sure the world remembered my mother and what she was forced to give up because of our Repopulation Act. But it never was. I never had the chance to right my father's ultimate wrong. Now I would finally be in a position to make the biggest difference. I just had to get this press conference over with.

Making sure to physically lean in my seat, I peer beyond my father's shoulder out into the garden. The do right by the son he worried he'd lost. To be honest, I probably would have made the same suggestion for similar reasons.

I had to keep the public on my side if I wanted to change their opinions on certain matters that were important to me. And having a caring relationship between the two of us, at least on the surface, was beneficial for both of us.

It had been so long since I'd spoken to so many people. I was surprised by the nerves I felt swirling in my stomach, and it wasn't just because of the tale I had to spin. So many years had passed since my first press conference that I had forgotten how it felt to be unfamiliar with this much attention. I couldn't help but smile to myself as I remembered the shake of my hands that first day. How I had to keep them stuffed into my pockets to stop anyone noticing.

They noticed, despite my attempt and thankfully saw my nerves as endearing, and so began my relationship with the public. I almost wanted to repeat that sequence of events today. I could feel my hands trembling slightly. But I wasn't the 'boy next door' anymore. I was to be President and the Settlement had to believe in my strength more than my likability right now.

My father cleared his throat, his restrained way of demanding my attention, and stood from his chair. He checked his watch before looking up at me.

"It's time."

determination that the State seek immediate retribution for my kidnapping, and his pride at me becoming President. As if he hadn't decided that would happen on the day I was born.

If everyone out there knew who he really was they would be shocked. As far as the outside world was aware, he was the friendly neighbourhood dentist. They had no idea he was 25% of the true ruling populous of our existence. No idea that he ordered the execution of the last President, the invention of the disease or the separation of Paige and Franklin. Perhaps the last point wouldn't garner the same level of anger as the first two; Paige wasn't as beloved as she once was. My father had made sure of it. It was up to me to change their opinion as best I could once I was safely sworn into office.

The reception in the garden did not sound the warmest and this only added to my nerves. I had suspicions that my father's story of my entrapment may not have held the weight with the public he'd expected and now I dreaded that I had been right. If I was right then that would make everything I needed to achieve even harder. My father turned his body towards me, held out his arms, and smiled. The cameras lapped up his show of paternal love but in all honesty, it made me cringe. Perhaps if he showed me that level of affection and care away from the glare of the lenses, I wouldn't mind so much, but now, it was all for show.

My father was not a physically affectionate man. He'd once patted me on the shoulder when I was upset but that's about the extent of the comfort and support

Control over every aspect of my life to make sure I achieved the highest honours.

I know that deep down, he hopes that after I become President, I will agree to take his seat on the board of the Téssera, but by the time my run in office is over, they will be more likely to assassinate me than welcome me into their ranks. I intended to use my stolen title to make as many changes to the Settlement as I could. Hopefully, they would be for the good but that's the problem with change - you can never predict the full ramifications.

Still, Bailey assured me that as long as decisions were made with light in your heart, then good would eventually come from them. I never had my aunt down as much of an empath but sometimes she surprised me. Maybe Paige's mother had been more influential on her than she care to admit. A part of me longed to meet with Di, my mother-in-law. She'd been such an intriguing figure for most of my life. Always there as background noise in my aunt's operations; an elephant in the room we never discussed.

I looked her up online more times than I cared to admit as a teenager. She was a wild woman and they're always the most interesting. It had only made my arranged marriage to Paige all the more appealing. I hadn't been completely sold on the idea until Bailey had informed me of her lineage. I hoped that in time, Paige would have opened up to me about what it had been like to grow alongside the mother of the Anarchists. Her actions though on the day of Paige's accident had accusations are flung my way. Instead, a light smattering of applause soon turned into a rapturous reception as I took my place centre stage, with Dad. There are happy tears at the corners of his eyes as he takes in the scenes around us.

Journalists have placed their notepads and recording equipment on their chairs so they can clap their hands together at the sight of me - the *prodigal son* returned. Eventually, they simmer down and order is restored but not before my ego has enjoyed the gentle stroking of their attention. I hadn't realised how much I missed the public adoration I grew so accustomed to in the run-up to my wedding. I'm not ashamed to say that I enjoyed this moment, especially after the last two years of days mostly populated with silence.

"Ryle, how does it feel to be home?"

"Ryle, are you glad to be back with your father?"

"What happened to your hair?"

"Are you okay?"

The questions come in rapid fire and I hold my hand up to slow them. I let out the warm laugh I'm known for and began to recite the story I'd told my father.

"Thank you all so much for coming out here today, and that welcome, well", I paused for dramatic effect, "I'm overwhelmed, to say the least. I know everyone is keen to find out what happened to me over the last two years and trust me, it's a story I can't wait to share. Now I can finally set a few things straight. I had a chance last night to read up on some stories about my

father's friendly façade flickers and I get a preview of
the rage that will await me once this conference is over.
Might as well enjoy the moment then.

"My wedding day was the happiest day of my life
and almost instantly it became the worst when I saw
Paige being flung into the back of a car outside the
reception. As any good husband would, I immediately
ran toward her, and that's the last thing I can remember
before waking up in a dark room alone. They moved
me from place to place regularly, always covering my
face as they did so. Once or twice I tried to steal a look
at them and received a beating not dissimilar to the one
you see me with now."

I make a show of rubbing the side of my stomach
as though it's a subconscious reaction to the memory of
the torture I'd been under. I know exactly what I'm
doing though. This will only work if they believe the
danger I was in.

"Many people have written about the theory that
Paige herself was behind my kidnapping but that
couldn't be further from the truth. Every single day I
asked after her and every single time I was ignored. I
only hope that she's out there alive somewhere and that
one day, she'll be able to make her way back to me. If
the good people of the Settlement hadn't taken it upon
themselves to attack that hut then I'm not sure I would
ever have made it back to my father alive. The fire was
the only thing that distracted them from the latest wave
of violence they rained down upon me, and in the
confusion, I was able to get away. I made it back to the

tide.

"If the person who has my wife is listening, then please, let her go. I know you acted rashly in an attempt to hurt me on the evening I became the President-in-waiting. I understand that emotions were running high. But please, she has nothing to do with that. The only thing she's ever done wrong was agree to take my last name. Let her go and we won't look for you."

There was silence as I finished my plea, making sure to look directly down the nearest camera barrel as I summoned all the emotion available to me. I was a man in love, desperate for his soulmate to be spared. My father's hand made its way up my arm and he squeezed my shoulder before pulling me into an embrace.

"Well played, son." he whispered before turning back to the crowd. "Now if there are no further questions, then my son and I would like some time alone. We have got a lot to catch up on."

He left the stage but I lingered behind him, desperate for a journalist to call out to me and delay the punishment that would be waiting back in the house after catastrophically stepping out of line like that. But no questions came. The press followed his orders and I watched as they departed from our garden. I only hoped that they and the people of the Settlement had bought my words and sentiment. Perhaps then I could start repairing Paige's reputation amongst them.

The boy, whose name he wouldn't share, wasn't forthcoming in any further conversation after his revelation about Ryle. My husband. The President. The State had him that much was clear, but if he was their figurehead, at least I knew he was safe. Or safe enough. I was desperate to know how it happened, what the public thought of him, and the lies that had been spun about his years on the run with us. But the boy wouldn't even grunt at me in response to my questions. Instead, he stared up at me through the floppy fringe of red hair that hung just in front of his eyes.

He consented to me checking his vitals regularly but that was the only interaction he would permit. The stench of fear and resentment lingered around him as he sat scowling in the corner of the shack. I offered him food and drink whenever I sought some myself and he took it without even a thank you or an acknowledgment of my presence.

The suns set and as our last candle flickered out, my thoughts were only on the day ahead. The day of infection for our only living test subject. I knew the boy's mind was on it too. In the darkness, I could hear him trying to quieten his tears.

"It's going to work," I offered him with far more confidence than I felt. He grunts in response, the most interaction he has granted me all day.

"It is."

"Is it?" There's no aggression in his tone, just vulnerability, and once again I am reminded of his youth. This boy should never have been allowed to

That wasn't to be his story though. If all went well he would become the first person alive immune to the disease. A beacon of hope for the Settlement and humanity. The first stand against the State that they couldn't undo.

"Yes, " I whispered.

"If it doesn't work tomorrow, will you do something for me?"

I regard his shadow through the light of the stars that seeps through the few remaining holes in the walls of the shack.

"Of course."

"Kill me."

His voice is ice cold. I'm sure he's never been more serious about something in his brief life. I want to make him this promise. I want him to draw some comfort from the fact I can offer him protection from the fate he fears. It will be a lie though. I have no intention of killing him no matter the outcome. I have too much blood on my hands already and I refuse to add this child's.

"Of course."

I repeat my last phrase, knowing the words are false as they leave my lips. If he picks up on my underlying thoughts, he makes no mention of them. My empty promise has brought him the comfort he needs and I listen as he lies down on the floor and pulls a blanket over himself. Soon the sound of his breathing becomes slow and soft, he's finally asleep. I'm not though. I can't keep my brain off the vial of the disease creating something like that.

As I fell into sleep I kept my thoughts tightly
around Leo and Violet, willing them into existence in
my subconscious so I could spend time with them.

I pictured the three of us leaving the hospital
together, sharing one car back to our home, ready to
spend the evening together. Leo is in the kitchen putting
together a spread and his famous lasagne Violet and I
make ourselves comfortable in the living room. We
exchange gossip and theories gleaned from the day
we've just had. I can almost smell the cheese sauce when
a knock at the shack door awakens me. Leo and Violet
snuffed out. It's already morning. It's already time

Elijio walks in and eyes the boy who's stirring
slowly from his sleep. In his hands is a hazmat suit
which he holds out towards me.

"You must wear this," he commands.

It's a ridiculous suggestion and will not help the
boy relax about what lies ahead of him.

"We do not know what the disease will do to you,
and until we do, this is safest."

He was right and with a sigh, I slowly pulled the
hazmat suit on. It crinkled with every movement,
nowhere near as comfortable as the ones Violet had
designed for the hospital. The mask didn't even have a
basic AI installed and it was at least two sizes too big for
me. Still, beggars can't be choosers.

I shuffle my way over to my cabinet and pull out a
glass. If the boy had to drink this concoction, then the
least I could do was provide him with a proper

I guess I was the one he had bonded with if you could call it that. I nod as best I can in the suit and he moves towards me, hesitating with his hand on the back of the seat. Run boy, run and I'll distract Elijio. The cure didn't kill you but the disease might. This could be your last chance to live.

"It will act quickly." Elijio's voice interrupts my silent desperate pleas to the boy to make his escape. The child nods at the Dweller and sits, his hand shaking as he grips the glass.

"Remember your promise."

He locked his eyes with mine, daring me to break the one thing giving him strength. But I will break that promise. I lied to him last night and now I let him believe the lie again.. I will not kill him. I cannot. I pray in that moment that the disease will kill him instead, so I don't have to betray him any further. With a quick motion, he throws his head back and pours the liquid down his throat. He slams the glass down as though he just finished a shot of tequila at a dive bar.

"Now what?"

"The fever should begin in two minutes, I accelerated the infection to save time."

Elijio is as a matter of fact as he always is. I can see his mind making notes of everything that has happened in the last few minutes; his way of making sure our findings are remembered and dissected should they fail.

The three of us watched the clock's small hand tick around the face. One minute. Two. Nothing. No cough, no sneeze, no slight drizzle of snot from his nostril.

on the floor."

The confidence in his tone that he'd first had on arrival is back and he almost lets a smile break out on his face.

"Can I go now?"

I nod and he stands up.

"You know where to find me if you start displaying any symptoms. I'll make sure everybody knows what you've done here for humanity."

"I just didn't want to kill nobody." He's modest, he doesn't realise that by volunteering he's saved countless lives and stopped the greatest evil the State had inflicted on its people. He just wants to get home and get back to his life knowing that his nightmares will never come true. He will never be responsible for anybody's death because of a mutation.

As he made his way to the door, he reached out his hand to pat Elijio on the shoulder. A way to tell him that there were no hard feelings between the two of them.

In an instant Elijio's hand was wrapped around the boy's throat as he pushed him up against the wall. It happened in a split second and I barely had time to stand from my seat before Elijio pulled a dagger from his pocket and placed it against the boy's throat.

"ELIJIO!" I screamed at him, taking the seven steps between the table and the two of them at a rapid pace. I tried pulling Elijio's arm backward but it was no use, I had no chance against him. A small trickle of blood was seeping from the boy's throat.

"I will kill you." He spoke to the boy, bringing his face so close to the child's that I was sure their eyelashes would brush against each other's. The boy squeezed his eyes closed and whimpered.

I need to do something. I need to find a weapon, I don't have much time. The dagger is pressing further into the boy's throat, soon it would make a cut that would matter. I retrace my steps back to the kitchen counter and pick up the glass, hurling it across the room at Elijio's head with all the strength I can muster. It smashes into a hundred pieces against his skull and he finally turns his attention away from the boy and towards me. He loosens his grip from the boy's throat and I hear the boy gulp in air and call out for his mother. Elijio lets him drop to the floor where he lays sobbing as he curls himself into a defensive ball.

"The cure worked."

He turns to look at me, pride in his eyes.

"What the HELL was that?"

I move to the cabinet to pick up another glass and throw it at Elijio. As it smashes against his chest, the boy lets out a whimper. I have to get to him. I have to get him out of here whilst Elijio is distracted.

"No Paige. You do not understand."

"I understand that you're insane. Get out of here!" I threw another glass at him as he walked toward me.

"The disease is triggered by adrenaline. The fight or flight technique you humans have."

I threw the last glass in the cabinet at him as he reached my position in the kitchen. I pulled the mask of front of me.

"I am sorry for what I had to do, at least now you know you are safe from your nightmares." He said to the boy without looking at him. His reassuring tone does nothing to heal the broken boy on the floor.

"Run." I order the boy who finally lifts his head from the floor. Elijio does not move to stop him as he pulls himself to a stand and hightails it out of the shack. His hand drags my arm away from the cabinet.

"That was unforgivable." I was furious with him and desperately wished to hurt him, but I knew it would be a fruitless use of my energy.

"And yet science will forgive me" he finally lets go of me and takes a step back. There is a sadness in his eyes but also a tinge of pride at having been successful. I hated him right now. Hearing the boy call for his mother had pulled at my maternal instincts, and thrown me into thinking about what I would have done had it been Franklin under Elijio's dagger. If it had been then we wouldn't be standing here talking in the kitchen. Elijio would have some implement or another poking out of him and I, would most likely, be taking my dying breath.

"I will be back when you have calmed down. Tonight I go to the lab to create more cure, then we plan how to save your people."

He walks out of the shack, leaving me simmering with rage and resentment. Despite how cruel his actions had been towards the boy he was right about one thing.

Science will forgive us.

Whilst Elijio was gone I had time to make up my mind about what I was going to do next. I'd decided I couldn't let him put anyone else through what he'd put the boy through, there was no need to. We knew the cure worked. As a scientist, I knew he'd want to run a few more tests to be certain that the boy wasn't an anomaly and logically, I knew it was the right thing to do. But I couldn't stop hearing the boy's desperate cry for his mother when he thought he was going to die. The tone of that one word had plucked at my heartstrings and rendered me unable to shut off my empathy any longer. What would I have done had it been Franklin pleading for me so desperately? I heard that word on my lips in some far-flung fantasy and wondered if my mother would feel as I did. Would she save me if my life was on the line?

No. She would not.

The people who had burnt our safe house to the ground were more than likely Anarchists, acting under her orders. She no longer cared if I lived or died, any maternal threads holding our relationship together had been severed. I wish I could say that it didn't hurt, knowing my mother had washed her hands of the love she once had for me, but I couldn't say that. The pain from her abandonment had taken root inside my bones, causing them to ache with childhood longing every time I took a step. There was a little girl inside of me, still desperate for her mother's approval. Still desperate for her mother to choose her over her beliefs. That little girl was dying now though, she had no hope left to cling to.

day we waited, more people developed mutations, and more families were pulled apart under the guise of completing their civic duties. More funerals were planned and more tears were shed. I wouldn't let it go on for a moment longer than it had to. When your inner child withers and dies, it changes you as a person. For some people, it makes them cruel, almost as if losing their childish innocence robs them of their soul. For others they mask the loss with humour and kindness, trying to put out into the world what they'd wished they'd received. For me, it made me more determined than ever to right the State's wrong. To create a safer world for Franklin.

I couldn't let my son grow up in a world where fear ruled his every movement. Where he would be signed up to die should he develop a mutation? I wouldn't let that happen to him. I wanted better for him. Isn't that what being a parent is truly about? Wanting to leave the world a better place for your child? Rus and Theo would make sure he grew into a fine young man and I would make sure he stayed alive long enough to achieve that.

It's been over two years since I last held my son on my wedding day. Some days, I struggle to remember what his voice had sounded like when we'd last been together. By now, he would have lost the babbling nonsense he spoke with. Now his lips would form coherently around words, his mind would be full of facts and questions that would help him make sense of the world.

his grandmother's legacy. All of that though, depended on the State allowing him to live and they wouldn't do that until I put a hole in their armour. Now Ryle was President though, perhaps my son would be granted leniency.

Ryle was a good man who had made poor decisions. I know he will do whatever it takes to ensure my son's safety after I've done my part. If my plan goes well, he might be welcomed back by the Settlement as the son of a hero. If it goes wrong, he'll be an outcast forever, forced to change his identity and name to avoid the crimes of his mother. Ironic really, that my son may end up following the same path I had.

I only hoped he realised I made these decisions out of love for him and not because of an egotistical need to be right. I may be tiptoeing the same justifications my mother took but I am nothing like her. I love my son and I will do anything I can to ensure his safety.

I don't bother trying to sleep. I knew my adrenaline would only keep me tossing and turning in my makeshift bed. Instead, I focus my nocturnal energy on packing anything useful I can find into my backpack. I hesitate over the laptop that's accompanied me on every step of my journey over the last two years. It holds the basis of the formula of the cure but if all goes to plan, I won't need to recreate it. Elijio and Bailey will take care of that. Besides, I need as much space in my pack as possible. I didn't know how much of the cure Elijio would bring with him in the morning and I didn't want to leave a single vial behind.

State's attention. I didn't want to have to hurt anyone but I knew I would if it meant the difference between success and failure. There were a lot of lines I was willing to cross today, I just prayed that fate didn't test me. I exchanged small talk with Elijio. He assumes my lack of warmth is due to my rage from the previous night and he wasn't wrong. I was still angry at him for the way he had treated the boy, the cruelty he had shown him.

It was disrespectful. The boy had volunteered his life to help our cause and Elijio had treated him like a plaything. It was because of his actions that I knew I was making the right decision; and that I would have very few regrets when I left this shack behind me. The only regret I had was the fact I might not get to see my son again. The odds were that whether or not I was successful, I would be captured by the State, which is why it was so vital I at least made this sacrifice count.

"You will meet your friends in a few days yes?"

"Has it been nearly two weeks already?" Time flies when you're sacrificing lives for science. In a few days, I was due to meet back up with Georgia and Ryle at the Waterfall. We were to reconvene and continue our life on the run, safe and sound once again. Would they still make the pilgrimage there after what I'm about to undertake? Would they still reach for each other without me as the glue binding their relationship together? I couldn't think about them right now. I couldn't consider their feelings or what the future would hold for them.

that this was all for him. To make the world a safer
place for him, to give him back the freedom he
deserves. Leo. Regina. Violet. Me. We've all sacrificed so
much for your safety kid. You are so loved and I hope
you grow up knowing that.

"I will be back this evening"

"With another test subject?" Please say no Elijio. If
you say no then maybe I don't have to do this. Maybe I
can bring you into the plan and increase my chances of
surviving it.

"We will see." Non-committal. Brilliant. "You are
okay for food?"

I nod. Despite how disgusted I was by his actions
last night, Elijio is a good person. He's done nothing but
try to help humanity the entire time I've known him.
Trying to save people who hate his kind because of lies
spun by the State. A bad person wouldn't behave like
that. A bad person would let us rot.

"Thank you" I want to offer him my gratitude
before he returns here to find I've betrayed him. He
places a case on the table and nods at me. It was too
risky for him to leave the cure in the lab until later and
he wouldn't risk his wife's safety by keeping it hidden in
their home. So he'd chosen the next safest place –
leaving it with me.

"It is my pleasure" he smiles at me and I can see
the hope in his eyes that I will forgive his actions. That
we will become close colleagues over the course of our
work and perhaps build bridges between our people
together. That smile will fade when he comes back

and then goes back inside. Without opening the case I put it into my backpack, tighten the straps around my shoulder, and take one last look at the shack around me. If you had told me three years ago that I would end my days sleeping on the floor of a makeshift shelter, I would have called you delusional. I had a beautiful house, a devoted husband, and a perfect newborn. My career was on an unstoppable trajectory and aside from a testy relationship with my mother-in-law, my days were carefree and full of friendly conversation with my best friend. It was the perfect life. I had been so lucky.

I walk out of the door and pause for a moment, listening to the sounds of the Dweller wildlife around me. It was like a chorus swelling in the wind, pushing me forward to complete my goal. Perhaps it was self-indulgent to see greater depth in the sounds of nature but it was what I needed to begin the walk back to the border. My first task was to make it through Nomad's land without being noticed. It wouldn't be too difficult as I'd grown up there. I knew the places one could tread without interruption. But then would come the fence. I didn't have a plan yet for how I would make it past that and into the main Settlement. The border to Nomad's land was at least a two-hour walk through Dweller forests from memory and after that, it would take me around three or four hours to pick my way through forgotten paths in Nomad's land itself. Plenty of time for logic to kick in and solve the problem of the fence.

As the shack disappeared into the distance behind me, I felt a wave of sadness curl itself around my body.

children are orphaned or parents burying their children? How many Dwellers would those with the mutation kill on the battlefield before we stopped them in their tracks? No. It was too many lives. Too many more deaths on my hands if I didn't act now. Acting now was the only option.

many, many obligations I had to undertake nearly hourly but I also had my own personal chef, so swings and roundabouts I guess. As I tucked into my chicken gyros, my mind drifted to Paige. Public perception of her was softening and I hoped that wherever she was, she'd noticed. When we meet back at the waterfall next week I want to put my hand on my heart and promise her she would be safe to return to the Settlement by my side.

No doubt my father would try all he could to scupper that plan but I'd given enough interviews now that touched on my love for her, that I was almost certain he could no longer kill her. It would be far too tragic a tale for people to withstand. Our morale was only just recovering from the first wave of the disease and all that it brought with it. The wedding had been a highlight in people's social calendars, and it was a slim beacon of hope they weren't quite prepared to give up on yet. Many journalists and members of the public had taken the time to approach me and express their sympathy for my predicament. They hoped Paige would make a safe return to me and that we could finally have the happily ever after that had been originally planned.

My father's PR machine had worked a little too well in the run-up up the nuptials and despite his best attempts, he was unable to undo the love he had sowed into the nation. Looking in my diary, I saw a 2 p.m. appointment with the devil himself pop up on my screen. With a sigh, my finger lingers over the keyboard. I could reject the meeting as I have done in the last few outside my door. It was James, my bodyguard. He was always lingering around me like an unpleasant smell, one that no doubt was emitted from the bowels of the Téssera. He was more of a spy than a security guard and I knew that if the time came, he'd probably be the one to implant a bullet into my brain. Still, he made pleasant enough conversation in the many, many hours we'd spent together so far.

I wished Georgia were with me. She would already have a plan of action in place, ready for the day I needed to ditch security to reunite with my friends. I couldn't very well allow him to come with me. That would be like walking a wolf into a barn. He would kill both of them before the public had a chance to see them again. It would be written off as a murder by the apparent kidnappers. No. The only way to keep them both safe was to walk them back into the Settlement myself. It would be harder to arrange an accidental death once we were all publicly reunited.

Still, that problem was a few days away whereas the conversation with my father was due to happen before the suns set. With a sigh, I open my desk drawer and pull out a notebook. I haven't had the time to put together a full dossier on all the changes I want to implement. Instead, I had more of a working list that spiralled occasionally into facts and figures. My father would put a roadblock up against anything I tried to put into law that went against his control over humanity, so I had to be sure that my plans were solid. He liked to undertake. I had decades' worth of indoctrination to unpick if I was going to make life safe and equal for all who lived in the Settlement. For so long the people who lived on Earth Two had been told that things had to be a certain way and I hoped that with just a few carefully chosen words, I could make them see things didn't have to be like this. I had to believe in myself and the strength of my convictions. I had to hope that others in the Settlement felt on some level as I did. I needed to be able to change hearts and minds with just a few well-chosen words to get others to believe in them.

We didn't have to breed if we didn't want to. We didn't have to sign up for the battlefronts. We didn't have to hate the Dwellers or anyone who loved differently from us. None of what we've been told since we've arrived has to be fact. The truth is subjective and my father has made sure to always bend it to his and his colleague's whim. I hoped most of the Settlement would secretly have thought like me over the years, not agreeing with the hate that the former President spewed but too afraid to stand up for what they believed in. I was going to give them a leader who would protect them if they stepped forward and denounced all they had been taught.

The first thing I had to do though was help Paige with the cure. Ridding the Settlement of the mutation would raise her in their estimations, and it would ensure that the Téssera couldn't create a super army to overthrow me when things stopped going their way. Because they would be furious when I started making bring a child into the world.

As they often did, thoughts of my mother led to thoughts of my aunt. Bailey had looked a lot like my mother back in the day. I'd seen a photo of the two of them together, just before she fell pregnant with me, and I could understand why sometimes people mistook them for twins. Bailey had been five years older than my mother at the time of the photo and now she was thirty-seven years older. It must be a heavy kind of grief to wake up every day and see the features of the person you had loved and lost, staring back at you in the mirror. Perhaps that's why she'd altered her appearance so dramatically with wild haircuts, piercings and tattoos. I was always so fascinated with her as a child. It was like a rainbow had walked into the room each time I was permitted to see her.

My father had tried to keep us apart but Bailey hadn't allowed it. Even then, she had a network of influence that could rival my dad's. Instead, she could visit me officially once a week. As I grew older and more independent, as my father's attention wavered, I saw her a lot more than the permitted allowance and I'm all the better for it. Other than a rotating roster of nannies she was the only person in the world who truly loved me and had nothing but my best interests at heart.

I checked my watch and pulled my jacket on, no time like the present to face my demons. I called out to the guard waiting at my door, to let him know that we were leaving. I might as well be seen playing along with the ridiculous measures my father has put in place. I

see another soul as I picked my way back towards the outskirts of human territory but all of that changed when I set foot onto Nomad's land. The quiet, unused pathways I'd played upon as a child were now a playground for a new generation of children and although they didn't pay me much attention as I weaved myself around their games, I knew they'd at least given me a passing glance. I just hoped the wanted posters the State had placed into everyone's subconscious no longer resembled me.

Thankfully these children were just like all others, too obsessed with their own entertainment to put the pieces together. Once again I longed for childhood, for a time when life was easier and my biggest worry was which book to read at bedtime. That period in my childhood had been short lived. It had existed in the brief gap between my father leaving and my mother taking up the mantle as leader of the Anarchists but it had existed and it had been wonderful.

There was one night in particular, I must have been about six years old when a meteor shower had been predicted. We spent all week learning about it in class but it wasn't due to illuminate the sky until nearly 3 a.m., so we were told we'd have to watch a recording of it in the morning. I'd gone to bed in a sulk, just as I'm sure all my other classmates had, but around 2 a.m., my mother climbed into bed with me and gently patted me awake.

"Agapi Mou, would you like to see?" she'd ask me.

moved through the pathways and into the more populated town-like areas. Once upon a time, I would have run through these towns laughing loudly with friends, not caring who I disturbed with my joy. Now I desperately tried to keep the weight of my determination from my face and shoulders, just as my mother used to tell me: *remain neutral and others will pay you no mind.*

A group of three elderly women sat on a porch and cast their eyes across me. I could feel their attention on the nape of my neck as I passed them.

"Paige?" One of them called out to me softly. On instinct, I paused in my walk. I had been made, and worse than that, I responded physically, only confirming their suspicions. I was frozen to my spot as I tried to work out what to do. I could run. There was no way any of those three could keep up with me. I could turn around and make sure they stayed silent. I didn't want to hurt anyone today. I truly didn't, but it was an option to consider.

A hand from behind me passed me a head scarf. It was dusty brown in colour but had golden thread intricately running through in a pattern of flowers and leaves. It was beautiful. I listened as the footsteps retreated away from me and without turning, I tied the scarf around my head, turning to look into a nearby window at my reflection. It had been a while since Georgia had cut my hair and my curls were showing more prominently than I realised. The scarf took care of them, and made me stand out less. Women in Nomad's land often covered their hair to keep the dust and dirt

They were on my side. I smiled at them, the tiniest piece of joy pulling at my mouth at somebody having faith in me. There were still people in this world who believed in me. There were still kind people in the world, people who could look beyond the State's lies and see the woman underneath them. They were the kind of people who would keep my son safe, who would welcome him back into civilization with open arms.

There would of course always be those who would try to prevent him from returning, people like Jack. People who had a grudge against his mother but I had to hope that kindness would outweigh hatred. Jack may be an exceptional lawyer, but without his good nature, he was no longer a master of the courtrooms. No matter how many injunctions he filed, or witch hunts he headed up, I had absolute faith that one day my son would be welcomed back in the Settlement. I had more hope than ever for Franklin's future after that moment.

I continued my journey towards the fence with renewed belief in myself and my plan. My plan. I still didn't have a plan to get across the border into the main Settlement. I'd been so focused on remaining invisible that I hadn't run the various scenarios through my mind and now I only had an hour or so to come up with a successful one. As I walked, I tried to clear my mind. Instead, it floated towards memories of Violet and Leo, as if they were walking alongside me toward my final destination. The two of them are silently talking with great animation about a topic I can't place. Probably because this is my imagination and not a memory. I here, then none of this would be happening.

I had made my decision though and the apparitions of my lost loves were just my brain going into survival mode. My story started with me being discovered by staff members next to the lake by the hospital, and that's where it's all finally going to end. My life will have gone full circle. I will go out undoing all the wrongs that I unwittingly helped put into the world.

My heart absolutely ached at the idea of never being reunited with Franklin. The maternal part of my mind screeched at me as I approached the fence, telling me over and over that I was being selfish. That I was behaving like the woman who raised me. That I was choosing my beliefs over my child, something I swore I would never do. But I still wasn't doing that. I was choosing life over my child. Life for him and life for others. I couldn't be further from my mother if I tried.

Just as I reached the gatehouse of the fence, a hand gently pulled at my arm. I whip myself around to face my captor. Ready to fight tooth and claw to escape but instead I was met with a familiar face. Carla. The human sympathiser who had helped us move between safe houses.

"Why can't you guys just stay hidden?" She smiles at me and lets go of my arm.

"Off to meet hubby?" She asks with a grin.

Clearly, she has a much higher impression of my relationship with Ryle than the reality. She must have watched the wedding live on her TV, maybe she'd even thrown a street party in our honour. To her, we were

I have a million questions I want to ask her but now is not the time. Soon Elijio would return to the shack and find me missing. He'd come looking for me, and he would stop me. I know he would. I couldn't let that happen. I had to get into the Settlement before evening set in. It would be harder for him to get to me in the main Settlement, not that I think Elijio would harm me in any way. All he's done for the last two years is help protect me, but I know that if he got hold of me, then he could simply carry me back to Dweller land. I wouldn't stand a chance.

"Need help getting across the border?"

"Yes please."

"I did wonder how long it would take you. You're earlier than I expected though."

"Old habit. If you arrive on time you're already ten minutes late."

It's the one lesson my father left me with - timeliness is close to godliness. I used to drive my mother mad with my insistence on always being early for everything. She was so laid back, I once heard her claim that time was a societal construct. But she used to give in to my pleas more often than not and we'd spend ten minutes killing time at every appointment or play date.

Back then she used to choose my needs ahead of her own, but as her work with the movement grew, she became less and less indulgent in my obsession with clock-watching until eventually I became used to always arriving late. The shame of it would burn on my cheeks

Eventually, I grew to enjoy weaving stories around others to achieve a preferred outcome but not when I was a child, not back then. Back then I needed honesty and stability, two things my childhood sorely lacked.

"Here, this should help."

In her hand was a blue identity chip, identical to the one I used to have to carry when I was a child.

"Tell them you have a shift at the printing factory. If they radio and ask, I've got a friend on the other end who owes me a favour."

The chip fits neatly into the small scar on my palm. The scar worn there by countless hours of gripping this stone in my youth, hoping somehow I could erode its existence, just with thought.

"Thank you."

She's far more resourceful than I ever gave her credit for. I always sort of assumed she was flighty, helping us with good intentions but no solid ideas of her own. An assumption I realise I made based on her looks. How chauvinistic of me. I should never have doubted Bailey's recruitment process' she only worked with the best.

"Don't mention it. I'll see you in a few days?"

Of course, we're supposed to return to Nomad's land to reconvene at The Waterfall with Georgia.

"Yes, definitely!"

I can hear the lie in my words but I don't believe she can; she's not listening for it after all.

"Take care of yourself, yeah? And go find your man!" She grins at me and winks, clearly, she thinks I'm

kind to me and it doesn't hurt me to let her believe in
the fantasy of my marriage. If things hadn't gone down
the way they did on our wedding day maybe I would
have believed it myself. I would have grown to love
Ryle. I know I would have.

She waves me off with a smile and I pull my
shoulders up. Now was the most dangerous moment in
my mission. If the guards at the gatehouse recognised
me, then it would all be over. I'd be executed before I
had a chance to explain where I had been. The last two
years of hiding would have been for nothing.

Thankfully, the guard doesn't even raise his eyes to
meet mine, too engrossed in the TV in his hut.

"Chip?" He asks with a grunt. I hold my hand out
and show him the blue stone in my palm.

"Fine. Go."

As I walk away from the hut and back into the
main Settlement, I can't believe how easy that moment
was. I try not to hurry as I move away from the guard's
hut. I'm supposed to be a woman on her way to work.
If I pick my pace up too much he might notice, he
might review the CCTV and recognise me. No, I had to
be slow and steady. I meandered towards my
destination, no matter how much my feet longed to
run.

With the guard hut now disappearing into the
distance behind me, I begin to walk faster. I had a lot of
Zones to get through and I didn't know what security
was like in the central zones now. At least with Elijio, I
knew what I was running from. Now I had no idea what

passed, paid me no scrutiny, one or two even shot me a friendly 'evening' as we walked in opposite directions towards each other. It was remarkable. If I hadn't been so focused on what lay ahead, I might have felt cocky, maybe called in at my local coffee store for a quick drink. My mouth salivates at the thought of it - it's been years since I had a decent coffee and the aroma of the shop is calling to me. I could be in and out in five minutes, my order wasn't a complicated one and surely after all this time I deserved a little treat.

Just as I was weighing up the pros and cons of a tiny detour, I noticed a woman watching me intently from the other side of the street. She wasn't trying to conceal her interest in me, instead, she was confident as her eyes devoured my appearance. The hairs on my neck stood to attention, my body instinctively telling me that this woman was dangerous, that she wished me harm.

With determined steps, she moved towards the edge of the pavement, meaning to cross the road to the same side of the street as me. I wasn't about to let it be that easy. The fact she hadn't started shouting to alert the authorities meant she wasn't working for the State which meant only two other possibilities - the Téssera or the more likely option, my mother.

I wasn't about to make it easy for her, not after I'd come so far. I pick up my pace and begin walking towards a destination that lingered in the back of my mind. I was in Zone Three now and despite the fact that most manufacturing took place in the outer zone, Zone steady, trying not to alert me to her presence. Silly rabbit. Doesn't she know the daughter my mother raised?

Stay calm. Keep your breathing steady. Never let them know you're afraid.

As I grew older my mother's lessons grew darker. She'd warn me of the dangers out in the world lurking just behind a stranger's smile. She taught me how to defend myself efficiently, but not so efficiently that a court of law could question the force behind it. Always let them leave at least one bruise, she'd advise me. It's much harder to argue against a physical sign of self-defence. Now that I have Franklin, I know beyond doubt that I had been too young for her lessons, not that she told me any lies about the world I was growing up in, but that she should have let my naivety fester a little longer, whilst I was still a child.

Then again, maybe if I'd had a daughter, I'd think a little differently. The world is different for a little girl.

Right now though, I wasn't judging my mother's parenting choices, instead I was grateful for them. The woman who had chosen to follow me did not know the magnitude of her mistake, not yet anyway. The little voice in my head, the voice of the woman I'd fought so hard to become, begs me to simply lose my stalker and carry on my journey. That's not possible though, the woman has seen me and if she reports back to her superiors then what I need to do will become even more impossible.

I wish we'd opened that bar. Or the restaurant. Or the bookshop. I wish we'd done anything other than continue being scientists. If we'd all quit seven years ago then all of this would have been avoided. But wishes are for children and the real world is for adults. This is my reality now and I'm finally growing used to it.

We're now only five minutes away from the factory turn-off. I wonder if she's figured out my destination yet. If she knows where we're heading and has an inkling of my plan to lead her into trouble. Judging by the fact her footsteps haven't once faltered, I doubt it. Capturing or killing Paige Hanson is far too good an opportunity to turn down. I wonder if I'm worth more to those hunting me dead or alive? Maybe I'll ask this woman in a moment.

She's maintained her distance from me so she obviously knows a little of my history. I would guess that she at least knows about my attack on Jack. Whether she worked for my mother or the State, his injuries would have been held up as a lesson in how dangerous I could be. It had felt so good at the moment happened to Paul. I can't recall any of the broadcasts I've overheard ever mentioning his name. He would be so heartbroken to have disappeared into obscurity. He'll be thrashing around in his early grave at the thought of it. Smiling to myself, I turn left onto the entrance walkway to the factory.

My path is blocked by a large woman. She's easily over six feet and her arms are swollen with muscles I wasn't sure even existed.

"You okay ma'am?" I nod at her in response and move to walk past her. "Can I see some ID?"

Once again, I've let my emotions get the better of my logic. Once again being my mother's daughter has been my undoing. If I'd just lost my pursuer at the first opportunity then I'd be closer to my end game, closer to salvation for the human race.

"I'm a Nomad," I offer her, allowing my voice to vibrate with the fear I'm actually feeling. Sometimes the best option to win people over is to show your genuine emotions. I taught myself that trick. "I'm, I'm supposed to do my first shift today."

There's a kind pity in her eyes.

"Do you have your chip?" She asks me softly, figuring it's her domineering physique that's causing me to panic. She's not entirely wrong. Clearly, she's another product of the disease's mutation. I wonder what she went through to cause this particular change.

I shake my head. She'll pay more attention to the chip than the guard, her pay grade assures me of that. She might even scan it and I don't know the

"You can wait in that hut behind me. I'll have a look around."

I feel bad, truly guilty for manipulating her like this. She seems like a good person, someone willing to help a stranger for no reason other than it's the right thing to do. Like the meek terrified woman I am half pretending to be, I walk towards the hut, open the door, and step inside. Now what?

All I've done is delay my inevitable discovery and arrest. That woman is at least twice my size and could easily crush me to death with those arms if I got on the wrong side of her. Plus, I've been sighted by the enemy. They may not be able to reach me at this exact moment but they've seen me. They know I'm alive and I'm back in the Settlement. It won't be long until the streets are crawling with others like her, all looking to collect their pound of flesh.

She opens the door far more gently than I thought her capable of and steps inside.

"I've checked around and I can't see anybody - do you know who it was you saw?"

"A woman. She followed me all the way from the Main Street."

She ponders this, clearly having wondered if I'd been being paranoid when I first told her I was being followed. She knows as well as I do, that only employees use this pathway to the factory.

"I'll check again when you leave for the day if you like. I can arrange a car to take you home as well."

able to fight back." Such a simple explanation but her eyes gave away the truth behind it. It hadn't been the first time that particular somebody had tried to hurt her.

"Now, I'm going to need to see your chip."

"I, uh, I'm not sure I'm comfortable going in for my shift now. Not after that."

I let my voice catch on my last few words and drop my eyes down to my hands as though I'm ashamed that being followed could scare me that much.

"Are you sure? If you don't show up then you might not have a job tomorrow?"

There's no malice or anger in her voice, she's stating facts, trying to get me to understand what's at stake. If only she knew what was truly at stake in this moment. If only she knew the real reason I needed to leave.

"I know, I know. But maybe they'll understand. I'll call them when I get home and explain. Would you mind if I told them about meeting you so they at least understand I made it here?"

"Of course. Did you want me to call you a car?"

I would love nothing more than for her to call me a car. But cars come equipped with monitoring devices, something I couldn't risk. I had to get out of the Settlement and rethink my plan of action. I would never make it to the hospital now. There would be too many eyes looking out for me.

"No. I think I'll be okay now. Hopefully, they've assumed I'm at work."

as much."

She chuckles and glances down at her hands, almost as if she's reliving the moment her mutation came to fruition. "Oh, I did. I most definitely did."

Time was against me now more than ever. I'd risked it all and failed. It wasn't feasible to pick my way towards the inner zones. It was safer to retreat with the cure back to Dweller territory until I could consider a new plan. Maybe Elijio would forgive me for leaving if I returned full of apologies. I knew he'd at least allow me to stay in the shack. He was too kindhearted to leave me to fend for myself in the wild. Besides, in just over a day, I was due to meet back at the waterfall with Georgia and Ryle. I wouldn't have to live with Elijio's cold shoulder for long. Just long enough to survive.

I kept my eyes trained on my feet as I walked with purpose out of Zone Three and into Zone Two. Thankfully, the factory I'd taken a detour to wasn't far from the border of the Zones. Within twenty minutes, I was safely across. One Zone down, two more to go. At this rate, I'd be back in Nomad's land after nightfall but hopefully before the evening's storm. As much as I had grown used to the scalding rain, I'd prefer not to add to my growing scars. I didn't know if it was my paranoia or self-preservation but I felt eyes upon me everywhere. Earlier today I'd enjoyed the sense of freedom of moving unnoticed through the world but now it felt as though I had a beacon over my head, inviting attention.

Logically I knew people would be hunting me, but I had to hope they'd start where I'd last been seen. Maybe they'd even waste time checking the factory to see if I was hiding there. It was a long shot but it was the largest piece of hope I had about my situation and I had to cling to it. I pulled the straps of my backpack from them.

"Paige Hanson has been spotted in Zone Three. All citizens must be on alert for her presence. Do not approach her, she is dangerous. Please allow the State's guards to apprehend her and return her to us."

So, they weren't planning on killing me immediately. I listened more carefully the second time the message was played, hoping to pick up something in Ryle's tone that let me know he was still on my side; that he still cared. But it wasn't there. Still, I was grateful that he wanted me brought in alive. I can't imagine that had been his father's initial wish. I didn't have long until a member of the public performed their civic duty and alerted the guards to my presence. I had to start walking quicker through the zones. Once I was back in Nomad's land there was a glimmer of a chance that somebody there would keep me hidden and safe. I just had to make it back there alive. If I was paranoid before the announcement, now I was definitely spiralling into dangerous mental territory.

It was impossible that everybody had frozen, with their eyes upon me but that's how it felt. I wish I had a weapon on me I could draw confidence from but naively, I'd set off from the shack without one assuming my trip to the lake at the centre of the Settlement would be uneventful. Georgia would never have come unprepared. She would have always had an emergency plan in the back of her mind, ready to take down anyone who stood between her and her goal. What would she do when we met back at the waterfall and I told her of

I wondered if I'd feel this sense of urgency if I hadn't been privy to the deaths of the test subjects and Elijio's treatment of the boy. If I'd stuck with my friends, would I have allowed Ryle and therefore Bailey, to dictate the how and when of distributing the cure? More than likely. I'd become a follower, not a leader recently. The last three years had dulled the fire in my stomach. They robbed me of the passion my mother had instilled in me long ago. Grief, guilt and circumstances beyond my control had turned me into a shadow of myself. It was nice to feel like myself again, even if I did tend to err on the side of rash decisions.

It would take about two hours to walk through Zone Two and then another three to get through Zone One and back to the fence guarding Nomad's land. My fingers moved to my pocket to check the identity chip Carla had given to me was still there. The inanimate object that had caused me so much rage and shame as a child was now a thing of comfort. If I can just keep walking without being spotted, then this chip would get me back to safety. Back to my friends. One step closer to being reunited with my son.

The Anesthesiologist who has held my hand with unwavering comfort throughout my surgery leans over my head and flashes me a cheerful smile.
"He's here."
I watch as fascination flits across Leo's features, as he peers over the cover that hides my abdomen from me, he's staring at our son. Our son who has yet to make a sound.

It's with that animalistic need in mind that my steps
pick up. Perhaps the universe threw this curveball in my
path to show me that there was a better way for all of
this to unfold. There was a way to save the Settlement
without sacrificing my own life. If I made it back to the
waterfall, back to my friends, then one day I could make
it back to my son. I could create the world he deserved

women are always trained by society to be small and unassuming. If I hadn't had such a fireball for a mother, I may have grown up that way too. But she always taught me to take up the space I needed in the world. To use my voice and to keep my mind sharp. No daughter of hers would be a yes woman or a cool girl. Her daughter would be a woman who changed the world, just as she had.

I wonder if mum knew just what the ramifications would be when she undertook that attack on the treatment centre. I wondered if she knew I wouldn't flee with her that night. If she guessed that her father's testimony would be the one that sent her to prison for life robbing her of any relationship with the child she'd loved so fiercely. Or had she just been so full of grief and rage over Kyan's disappearance, that she'd stopped caring? Just for a brief moment, she let herself act without thought to what the consequences could be.

Surely she couldn't have worried about losing me, as she stuck a knife in the first guard's eye. In her warped mind, at that moment, she was doing it for me, she was brutally killing and torturing those guards **for me.** To avenge the loss of a man we both loved. To create a world that was fit for her child. Or at least, that's what she told me over and over in the letters I never returned. Grandpa Joe would always give them to me when they arrived, but I could feel his relief as I threw them away after reading them. He didn't want me to crawl back into her web. He wanted better for me and he made sure that I got it.

choice. My heroic act would have granted him freedom but I would never have expected thanks for it. I would have respected the pain it would cause him. I would have been nothing like my mother. I am ***nothing*** like my mother.

Halfway through Zone Two, I notice a man pull out his phone and aim it in my direction. I heard the snap of a camera shutter and the whizz of the tone as it was sent off to somebody. A friend of his? The State? Whoever it had been sent to was bad news for me. It meant my movements could now be tracked. The Agents hunting me would now expand their search into this Zone, maybe even figure out where I was heading.

Time was ticking loudly all around me and all I could do was run.

Shit.

That's the only word that's running through my mind as one of my advisors stands before me, brandishing a tablet. On that tablet is a video of Paige walking through the streets of the main Settlement. He's watching me for my reaction, ready to report back to the powers that be on how I took this news. As to what team I was truly on. It wasn't time to show my cards yet, I had to be smarter than them. So far my public support of Paige has been explained away as a PR strategy. I wasn't prepared to tell them any different yet.

"We need to get an alert out onto all of the public systems."

I take my eyes off the screen even though every inch of my skin aches to keep watching her.

"I'll record the address immediately. Have them prep the studio."

I've passed the aide's test and he smiles at me tightly as he takes the tablet back and turns it off. I want to snatch it out of his hand so I can watch Paige as she moves through the Settlement, so I can make sure she's safe, but to do so would alert suspicions that are already lurking beneath the surface. I convinced my father and his colleagues that my outburst at the press conference was a clever ploy to garner more public sympathy and that it had nothing to do with Paige or my feelings towards her. I was, after all, just following the designs of their grander scheme. The one they'd put in place when they'd told me of my engagement to her, to win public

In reality, I had to win as much public affection as possible to keep the people on my side when I went against the Téssera and their wishes. It's far harder to arrange the disappearance or death of a popular public figure, and I was destined to be the most popular one in living history if the polls were to be believed. People were still captivated by the love story behind my marriage. They still wanted to witness our happily ever after despite all the lies that had been spun about my wife. My wife. I call her that now and then and I have to say it doesn't feel foreign on my tongue.

One of my biggest regrets in life will always be the lies I told Paige to keep her safe. I wish I could have just been honest with her from the outset. I should have told her I knew about her heritage or of her mother's involvement in her accident. I could have clued her in on the actual reasons as to why I agreed to the marriage. But Bailey had assured me I couldn't. She told me that Paige was an unknown entity, she could end up being just as emotionally charged as her mother. My aunt had never meant for the massacre on the treatment centre to happen. I truly believe that.

She told Di about Kyan's demise on the understanding that they would work together to plan out a raid, that they would take their time with the information to make sure retribution was won at the lowest cost of life. She had been just as shocked as the rest of the Settlement when she'd seen the news footage of Di standing to the side of the burning treatment centre, screaming out in a mix of joy and anger.

But Di didn't care to hear about their innocence, she just wanted their blood as payment for the Dweller she loved. Some days I could almost understand the logic behind her madness, however childlike it truly was. Somebody hurt you so you must hurt them. I'd never admit that to my aunt though, she'd worry about the darkness that kind of thinking could invoke.

The more I got to know Paige the more I saw how different she was from the woman who raised her. Yes, she was an emotionally charged individual, but she was a logical creature, at the end of the day. She'd played along with every one of Paul's games to achieve her goal - to be reunited with her son. The hoops he made her jump through, mostly the marriage to me, must have killed her emotionally. She was still in the grips of mourning Leo when I was forced to put a new diamond-encrusted promise on her finger. But she handled it with grace. She didn't fly off the handle in the way her mother had. She was better than that. And even if, as I was starting to suspect, she had meant to push Paul as hard as she had I couldn't blame her. I'd wanted to kill that man on more than one occasion myself.

The more time I spent with her, the harder it was to agree to my aunt's warnings that she wasn't to be trusted to manage her emotions. I rarely disagreed with Bailey on things but Paige had become a bit of a rubbing point in our relationship so we spoke about her less and less as our courtship took its well-plotted course. It wasn't until Bailey got wind of the escape plan that we began to be on the same page again about the

plan would have gone off without a hitch. None of us
would have spent the last twenty-four months living like
outcasts, moving from house to house at the slightest
twitch of paranoia. Not that I wasn't grateful to Bailey
and her team for keeping us as safe as they did, but the
constant moving meant we could never put down real
roots together. The three of us were never really able to
stay still long enough to process all we had been
through. I guess the time for healing would come soon,
although not at the appointed time now Paige has gone
off script. What the hell was she doing wandering
through the Settlement? Why couldn't she just have
stuck to the plan and met us at the Waterfall as we
agreed on the night we parted in the woods?

I was beginning to think that whilst Paige might
not share her mother's violent tendencies, she certainly
shared her habit of running into situations without a
fully formed plan. I wondered what Georgia had made
of the news. I knew she hadn't been captured yet as that
would have been included in one of my daily morning
briefings. I would have been expected to address the
nation regarding her capture or death and, so far, her
name hadn't made the lips of any of my aides, so I knew
that wherever she was, she was safe. I hoped she was
smart enough to stay that way, once news of Paige's
escapades were made public.

There was a knock at my door, signalling that the
recording booth was prepped and ready for me to
record the alert that would be immediately broadcast all
around the Settlement. I knew exactly what my father

different words, ones that were softer, and calmer. Ones that were simple and efficient, but most importantly, ones that would keep Paige alive until I could work out a way to get her out of this mess and safely back by my side, as my wife. You can't very well kill the wife of the President when the two of them have finally been reunited, can you?

Besides, if I were to get on those speakers and demand her head, it would undo all the positive public opinion I'd been so busy courting and the Téssera wouldn't want that. If the public isn't on our side then they lose their influence. I make a mental note to bring that point up in the debriefing with my father, which will no doubt be booked in the second my alert goes live.

I stand up with firm shoulders and a serious look on my face. I need everyone who looks at me to see a man on a mission. A man who has nothing but the Tessera's best interests at heart, because who knows how many moles my father has planted in my office building. More than a handful, I'd guess. No, to anyone paying attention, I had to be playing the part right now, until it was too late to stop or change my words.

"Is this a live broadcast?" I ask the aide who is scurrying alongside me.

"No sir, it will be broadcast two minutes after recording."

"Two minutes? Do you think we have two minutes to waste in this situation? I want it live."

my seat in front of the microphone and watch as he presses buttons. I'm surprised he hasn't tried to sneak away and make a call to my father to confirm my request. Perhaps he's hoping that by following my orders, we'll capture Paige quicker and deal with the thorn in my father's side. Maybe there's a bonus he's had his eye on for a job well done. Whatever the reason, I'm grateful for his compliance as the light above his head changes to red to let me know I will be speaking live to the nation.

"Paige Hanson has been spotted in Zone Three. All citizens must be on alert for her presence. Do not approach her, she is dangerous. Please allow the State's guards to apprehend her and return her to us."

I emphasised the word return. I want it to be implicit that I want her returned to us alive and unharmed. By painting her as dangerous it might spare her from any vigilante justice citizens might dole out in memory of people they have lost to the disease.

My aide's face pales as he realises I've deviated from the agreed script set out in front of me. Just as I suspected, my father wanted to offer a reward for her capture or untimely death. By any means necessary had been the phrase he'd wanted me to use. Surely by now, my father knows I'm always going to go my own way when it comes to this particular woman? The press conference, upon my return, should have shown him that.

I stand up from my chair and move to the corridor where I can hear my voice echoing around the streets.

always wanted to create for the President. Some of those agents, like Georgia, were good people who genuinely believed they worked to keep the people of the Settlement safe but others were nothing more than ill-tempered puppets of the Téssera and I knew which kind I'd rather Paige encountered.

My watch beeped to let me know I had a new appointment, just as I knew it would. A meeting with my father at the family home.

"The car is outside" the aide informed me through a thunderous expression. I almost felt bad for misleading him. Almost.

I kept up a light jogging pace as I moved through Zone
Two into Zone One and mostly everyone paid little
attention to me. I was surprised the State was taking this
long to react to my presence. Perhaps my husband was
delaying them as much as he could. Surely, after all
we've been through together, he wouldn't want me
captured. Not really. Not when he knew what we were
working towards.

Although he was President, now he was secured in
his father's pocket, maybe he no longer had any choice.
I felt sorry for Ryle. At least my mother, despite her
more bloodthirsty moments, had loved me. His father
had never flashed him anything more than a passing
glance. Ryle was a valuable commodity to his dad,
nothing more.

As I was keeping my head down and my feet
moving, my focus was whipped from the sidewalk
toward a familiar voice.

"I didn't do shit."

The boy was being manhandled by two State
Agents. He was throwing his whole body weight against
them in an effort to get away from the car they were
trying to cram him into.

"I'm not going anywhere with you."

As he spat onto their shoes, his eyes met mine over
their shoulders.

My feet froze in panic. This was it. This was the
moment everything fell apart. We shared eye contact for
a moment and I waited on him to inform the agents of
my presence. They'd let him go in a heartbeat to

person. At least I saved this boy who was about to send me to my death.

"I told you, I ain't going with you."

He stamped on one of the agent's feet hard. I could hear the cracks of bone from where I stood behind them and I winced. The other Agent ignored his friend's injury and turned the boy around into a position where he could twist his arms behind his back. The boy cried out in pain but still, he did not alert them to my presence. Still, he kept me a secret. I send a silent prayer of thanks to the sky and go to carry on my journey. This boy has given me my freedom and I would be a fool not to take it.

Unfortunately for the logical side of my brain, the emotional side won, as always. My feet moved. But not away from the scene before me and towards Nomad's land. Instead, they stepped toward the two Agents who were unaware of my presence. The one with the injured foot was easy to take down, a swift punch to the back of the neck sent him down in a heap towards the ground. I should check if he's breathing. I should put him into the recovery position. That's what a good Doctor would do.

I am not a good Doctor.

Not anymore.

His colleague would prove to be a little trickier and I wasn't quick enough as his hands found their way to my neck. I fought back the panic in my bloodstream as I tried to hook my fingers under his palms. I just needed to create a tiny amount of room to free my windpipe. My breathing was coming out in silent gasps as the trail of sticky blood coming from the side of his head. The boy offered his hand to me as he dropped his makeshift weapon. He pulled me to my feet. I tried to thank him but my throat was so tender it hurt to breathe. I have enough brains in my head still to remember to grab my backpack from the street where it had fallen, and together we move away from the two agents, in silent hurried footsteps.

"Thanks" he offers me with a half-smile. There's still resentment lingering underneath his features but he has obviously forgiven me enough to save my life. A high-pitched siren sounds from the speakers around us. I guess that one agent has made it to their panic button and alerted the authorities to the attack on them. We have five minutes, if that, to get to safety.

A woman appears at the door of a house just in front of us. She stares at us before glancing around the street. Maybe we have less than five minutes now there was a witness. I'm sorry Franklin. I couldn't make the world a better place for you. I tried. I really did.

Thoughts of my son flood my brain and I'm full of regret, words I'd never get to say to him, moments I'd never get to share with him. A normal life that our decisions stole from him. I wish I could tell him how sorry I was that this was how our story ended. Not for a moment in the delivery suite did I imagine a life where the three of us weren't together. He was never supposed to be alone.

I should have known though, that the universe likes the poetry of life turning full circle. My parents frustrated. Was this his plan all along? To hand me in himself to claim the reward? Can't say I blame him after everything he's been through. I look at his face as he holds my hand pulling me forward towards the front door. He's so young, too young to be taking on this responsibility and this guilt. Too young to hold my life in his hands.

"Hurry" calls the woman to us in a whisper that carries its way through to my heart. Its tone is friendly, and full of concern. Perhaps she is not the enemy. I want to ask the boy questions, but my throat is still swollen from the agent's grip.

"Safe?" That is all I can croak out to him. He turns to look at me, finally letting go of my hand as he takes the first step towards the door.

"Safe." He replies with a smile, gesturing for me to follow him. Perhaps I'm too bleak in my assessment of fate and the universe, maybe it wants me to break the cycle. Maybe it wants me to succeed.

I follow him inside and the woman is standing in front of a wardrobe. "In here" she urges opening the doors to it and sliding a panel in the back. The boy climbs in and I follow suit, trying to smile at the woman who's aiding us but grimacing instead as I push my way through coats into darkness. Almost silently she closes the panel and locks it. We're alone and the air is so black I can't see my hand in front of my face.

It's a human compulsion to feel uncomfortable in the dark, it's an instinctual fear of the unknown. Where our overactive imaginations give more meaning to every room until I began to cry, then she'd light it again and take me into her arms. Pointing out that the landscape around us hadn't changed in the slightest, we were still home, we were still safe, and the only thing that had changed was my ability to see that. Each time she blew out the candle, I could go longer and longer without her comforting touch, until eventually it became almost second nature to sit on the basement floor with nothing but my thoughts to light up the world around me.

The boy doesn't seem to be fussed about the darkness around us, his breathing has remained stable and I hear him move to sit on the floor. There's no pacing or nervous tics to notice. I wonder, for a moment, if his parents put him through the same childhood exercises my mother had before realising that was highly unlikely. Nobody else had a mother like mine. I feel the floor with my hands and guide myself into a sitting position near to him. I can feel the heat from his skin and smell the drying sweat from our recent exertion together.

"Now?" I ask him in a whisper, still unable to formulate more than one word at a time without pain stroking my vocal cords. I'd have a hefty bruise forming around my neck soon.

"We wait. They'll check each house in the area and if we're lucky, they'll expand the search to further afield and we can move." His voice is low and soft, the immaturity I'd heard in it back in the shack has vanished. This boy now has a new purpose, I just wasn't sure what it was.

from them is the right thing. I'm not going with them, no matter what. I'd rather fucking die."

Now he was sounding more like the boy I'd met at the shack. Full of anger and resentment. We sit together in silence as we wait for the sound of footsteps to appear just the other side of the wall.

"They've built a school," he offers and I wait for him to expand on his words. Pushing him wouldn't get me any further information. I'd learnt that from our time together.

"A school for kids like me. Ones whose chips are green. They're rounding them all up and carting them off to a school in the central zone. For training, they've said. They don't get to come home though. They want to take my little cousin, she's six man. She should be living at home, playing with her toys, and asking questions sixty times a day, not training to fight in the war. I got her away though. My aunt had agreed to the collection, can you believe it? Said it was her civic duty. Some mother she is. I snuck her out in the night though, they'll never find her in Nomad's land." His story was painting a picture for me that I'd heard about but had tried not to consider too deeply.

A world in which children who will mutate belong to the State. Once again, they were hiding their truths under the guise of people undertaking their civic duty and the fear of what going against that would mean.

This is a new level of Spartan bullshit.

to be one of the worst. I'm in an actual time-out.

Banging my fists against the door, I take pleasure in the wood's movement beneath my anger, but I know nobody is coming to let me out. Not until Anton the Great deems it acceptable. I've been in here for hours now. The car that picked me up for our supposed meeting had locked its doors automatically once I was seated and then it had driven at breakneck speed to this house I now find myself trapped in. A strange gas had been emitted from the car's console and no matter how many times I jabbed at the window controls, they wouldn't open. And then I woke up in this room with a bottle of water. He wasn't a monster after all. There was also a simple note on my father's stationary:

You need to learn to behave.

That was all he'd written to me in his snake-like handwriting. I used to be fascinated by the way he wrote letters growing up. The words always seemed so adult written in his personal font but now I saw them for what they were: a distraction. A way to keep up the charade that he was nothing more than the friendly neighbourhood dentist. After all, doctors always had ineligible handwriting so why would dentists be any different?

I had always wondered why he chose dentistry as his fabled profession when he could have chosen any career he wanted. Perhaps it was something about pulling teeth that appealed to the darker side of him but I'll never know because I'll never ask him.

we must have spoken about something other than
political ambition but I'm unable to recall the
memories.

I can't believe he's locked me away like this. Left
me alone to learn my lesson. What is he hoping to
achieve? That I'll emerge from this temporary
imprisonment full of regret and apologies? He taught
me better than that. To say sorry shows weakness. A
man must always stand by his convictions, regardless of
the consequences. I wouldn't do that. I would stay in
this room until he decided I'd learnt my lesson and that
would be the end of it.

It's been so many years since he's employed this
punishment tactic, that I'd almost forgotten my coping
mechanisms. Back then, my imagination was more vivid
and I was able to keep myself entertained with thoughts
of a fantasy world in which my mother was alive. She'd
come charging into the house, knock my father to the
floor and steal the key to the door from his desk. I
hated that key. It was so heavy and ornate. Every time
his hands hovered near it my skin would prickle
knowing that time in the room was due.

I told myself many times growing up that one day,
I would be too big for him to lock away. That one day I
would be the one to push him into the room upstairs
and lock the door. He would know what it was like to
be left alone with nothing but his own thoughts for
company. I wondered if eventually, the solitude would
bring any guilt to the surface over his actions over the
years. If I left him long enough would he be driven mad

control. To him, it was parenting. To the rest of the world, it would be seen as neglect.

Bailey never knew about these trips to the locked room, she didn't even know of its existence. It was on the very top floor of the house, a floor nobody ever needed to visit. I didn't tell her about the punishment because I knew, even as a child, that if she found out she would make my father disappear. And as much as I didn't like my father, I didn't want him gone from my life forever. A sentiment that was easing as I aged. I'd been naive to think he'd have boarded this room up on the day I moved out, that he would have no further use for it. I wonder if by now this room has had occupants that weren't me. Judging from the disused state of it, I would guess not but I wouldn't put it past him.

I ran my hands over the floorboards, feeling the grooves my younger fingernails had dug in them. There, underneath the seat of one of the chairs, was the rude poem I'd scribbled down one of the few times I'd smuggled a pen in here with me. If I knew I was due a lesson up here then I always tried to bring contraband with me. Something to help me pass the time. Sometimes I'd only be up here for an hour but other times it felt like I wasted whole days trapped inside these four walls. If my father intended to teach me a message today it was failing, however. All he was doing was allowing me a walk down memory lane.

He may have seen this room as punishment but in a lot of ways this room became my form of escapism. Here in this room, I could be anyone, I could do

to save Paige and Georgia. There would be nothing
beyond my means when I was finally permitted
freedom.

I sit on the floor with my knees raised and my head
leaned back against the arm of the chair. I always chose
to sit like this. Sitting on the seat felt like accepting
kindness from my father in those moments, and
kindness bred caring and I never wanted to care about
my father when he locked me in this room. I'd wager
that this seat is the only item of furniture that has never
needed replacing due to wear and tear. I wondered if it
bothered him that I disregarded his olive branch. Then
realised I cared about his feelings as much at this
moment as I did as a surly sixteen-year-old. Or a
confused ten-year-old. Or a frightened five-year-old.

He tried to make me see that it was my fault that I
had to be locked away. All I ever learnt from these
moments though, was how to play the part, what to say
and do to appease my father and those around him. In
some ways he was right. Being confined in this room
did always teach me a lesson. Just never the ones he had
in mind. I remember being locked in here for an entire
afternoon, once, when I was about thirteen. We had
been sat eating lunch, in silence, when I tried to
approach the subject of attending a local school. A
proper school with friends my age and a curriculum that
would match my peers.

He'd told me no but I'd pushed the point. Tried to
reason with him. In return, he marched me up the stairs
and left me until the suns set. He said it was to give me

my childhood prison, I reflected on the many other times I'd been forced in here. Resentment began to simmer inside me as I thought of the hours of my life that had been wasted atoning for sins that didn't matter. My father had no right to treat me that way. No parent, no matter how emotionally stunted, should treat their flesh and blood that way. It had been wrong. It has taken me over thirty years to cement that fact in my brain. Sure I'd flirted with the fact that my upbringing wasn't normal but this is the first time I've truly admitted to myself that it wasn't right. Nothing about my childhood had been right.

Two days after I left home I booked myself in for a secret procedure. The snip they used to call it on Earth one. Here we call it being a criminal of the State. So I knew I'd never be a father. But if by some chance of fate, a child came into my life one day, I would be sure to do everything right. I wouldn't dish out cruel punishments. I would hold them tightly when they hurt themselves or were afraid. I would get onto the floor and join in with whatever imaginary world they'd created. I'd make sure they felt loved from the moment they awoke until the moment I tucked them in for the night. I'd laugh at their inane jokes, show interest in their hobbies and above all else, I would respect them as a living being. In short, I would be the father I never had. The father that every child deserves.

Thankfully, I never regretted my procedure, never had the paternal longing to create a miniature version of myself but that didn't stop me from promising the

Georgia return to civilisation. I wondered how Paige
and I would play out the rest of our relationship. The
problem with public opinion being very much on our
side was that I wasn't sure how they would take it if we
were no longer together. But I couldn't very well force
her to stay married to me if she didn't want to.

I was ashamed to admit that there was a part of me
that wished I were the type of man who would force her
to stay by my side. I grew used to her company, no
matter how sullen it had become. I learnt how to make
her coffee to suit her mood for the day. Three sugars
and a dash if it were a normal morning, four sugars and
a glug if she hadn't slept. Despite the shadow of herself,
she'd become, I could still remember the bright and
vivacious woman she'd been when I first burst into her
life. She was, without doubt, one of the most resilient
people I'd ever met. Nothing life or the State threw at
her had broken her, and I wanted to make sure they
never got the chance to hurt her again. I cared for her.
Probably a touch more than I ought to. Our relationship
had, after all, been a means to an end. A way for us to
both achieve our goals.

Hopefully, she wouldn't divorce me immediately
but I would understand if she did. I must be a constant
reminder of Paul and the control he had had over her
life for six months. I'm sure though, given how
amicable our relationship had once been, that she'd help
me manage public perception of our split to ensure the
best outcome for us both. It would do neither of us any
good for the public to feel that they had to pick sides in

coming up the stairs towards the doors and decided to act rashly. In all the times my father locked me in here never once did I fight back but right now my hands were itching to hit something and my father's face seemed an attractive target. The door opened inwards so I crept as swiftly as I could across the floor boards until I was standing just to the side of the door frame. My plan was an emotional one, one I would regret, but one I would also enjoy. The second he swung the door open, I would pivot from my hiding spot and extend my arm. I'd make sure not to use enough force to cause any lasting damage, I didn't want to actually hurt him. Did I? No. I just wanted to show him he couldn't bully me anymore.

The door opened with a creak and before I had control of my emotions, I swung towards him, as hard as I could. Years of resentment contained in my fist. As I connected with his face, regret washed over me. Because it wasn't my father. It was just one of his aides.

"I had a feeling you might be in a bit of a mood."

He was standing at the bottom of the staircase, confident that the fight would have left my system now and he wasn't wrong. The shock of hitting someone innocent had calmed me in an instant. He was always one step ahead. I took the steps towards him slowly one by one, hoping that my rage would return the closer I got to him. But it didn't. It was spent. And unfortunately on the wrong person.

They wouldn't stop. They would never stop.

I could make everyone in the Settlement immune to their disease. I could cure everyone currently infected but it would never be enough. They would never stop controlling every aspect of our lives and would always work on another way to win the war that they actually started. They had no qualms about murdering their own troops to justify starting the war all those years ago and their disregard for human life has only grown since then.

They were greedy and greed is dangerous. It can never be truly sated, always there waiting to rear its head again and ask for just one more. Just one more piece of chocolate. Just one more coin stolen. Just one more life taken.

No. It would never be enough. I wasn't thinking big enough with this plan, the cure would only be a slight inconvenience to the members of the Téssera. The ones who hide behind the cloak of democracy, who pretend we have a say in the trajectory of our lives. They only ever do what suits them.

The invention of these schools, telling parents it was their civic duty to send their children away to be trained and then killed, was a sign of just how twisted their minds were becoming. What next? What could they possibly inflict on everyone next?

The boy is staring at me as we sit together in the dark behind the false wardrobe door, waiting for a response from me. Some acknowledgement that I've heard his confession. I'm aware of the horror the State, up, with shorter gulps of air as his heart rate increases. Mum always said that darkness held an advantage if you just learnt to embrace it and she wasn't wrong. Right now, I was picking up on numerous tells from the boy that his fight or flight instinct was being triggered. I hoped he wouldn't do anything rash because of it. Adrenaline can often cloud judgement.

I listen with enhanced attention to the voices above us. Two males and the woman who had ushered us inside the house. Her tone is friendly and concerned, just another good citizen partaking in her civic duty by allowing the State to search her home. They aren't light in their touch as they move their way around the home above us. I hear their stomping footsteps and heavy hands on her belongings and more than once, I hear a thud as they drop something to the floor. There are no apologies or words exchanged with her as they look for us in every nook and cranny.

Their footsteps linger outside the closet and I have to resist the urge to position myself on the other side of the concealed door. My body wants to ready itself for a fight should they find us, but in moving I could give our position away. I hear the creak of the closet door opening and hear their hands shuffling through the coats it contains. Please don't find the latch. Please don't find the latch.

The noise of shuffling clothes fades and I hear the closet door close. I count to a hundred after I hear the front door close before I give the boy's arm another comforting squeeze.

149

Tomorrow. I can't wait until tomorrow. I'm supposed to be at the waterfall meeting up with Georgia and Ryle. I'm supposed to be distributing the cure to the Settlement and saving lives. Not cowering behind a wardrobe from the very people I need to protect humanity from.

"No."

"Yes." He responded, his voice growing in volume before he caught his temper.

"Somewhere to be."

Those words are gradually getting easier. I wasn't sure if it was recovery or rage that was numbing the pain after what the boy had told me about the schools and the snatching of children. My mother's blood was pumping through my veins again. I couldn't let them do this.

The State, the Architects or the Téssera, whatever you want to call them - they've taken everything from me. They've taken my husband. My son. My best friend. My mentor. My career. My home. My happily ever after. I can't let them continue doing this to people. I can't let them continue destroying lives to appease themselves. I won't.

"No." He replies again, pulling himself back onto his feet and pacing away from me.

Something inside me snaps. For three years now everyone else has been running my life. Telling me how to behave, what to say, how to act and what my aims should be. I've had enough. I won't listen to anyone else's orders anymore.

order me to play the part. To stay in line. I wasn't going to be the good girl they all wanted anymore. I would not be the grieving widow, the perfect scientist or my mother's daughter anymore. I was going to be Paige. Just me.

The woman pulls the door open hesitantly and I push my palm onto the gap, forcing it open further. I can feel her trying to push it closed again. I know that this behaviour is fuelled by emotion and not logic. I know that behaving like this will put her and the boy in danger for helping me but I can't care about that right now. Right now, I need to get out of this house and away from these people. It's safer for them if I'm not around.

I pull my backpack tighter and shoulder barge the door open. The woman stumbles backwards under the force but thankfully she doesn't fall to the floor. My aim hadn't been to hurt her but I had bigger fish to fry now. Even if I got the cure into the water supply, it would never stop the Téssera. It would just delay them. There was only one way they could be stopped and there was only one person who could help me.

"Do you know Bailey?"

It's a question I shouldn't need to ask. That woman's web clung to the air all around the Settlement but I still needed confirmation. The woman regains her composure and nods, the determination in my eyes robbing her voice of its power.

shot to keep me hidden behind the wall. To keep me safe whilst he follows Bailey's plan. It wasn't going to happen though. I couldn't be talked down and I didn't fear him physically.

"Please stay."

He's taken a tactic I hadn't expected, he was showing me he actually cared. The tone of those two words is soft and pleading and they pull at my maternal heartstrings. He's a child who just wants the best for me. Part of me wants to stay. It would be so easy to stay and overlook the evils the Téssera are consistently unleashing on the population.

Then I think of Leo's expression as we flew through the barrier into the lake. I can see Rus being marched to the gallows. I hear Franklin's screams as we were shot at by Government Agents. I can imagine Regina's gasp as the bullet hits her and she falls to the floor with Franklin in her arms - desperately trying to shield him from the impact even in her last moments. Finally, I remember the warmth of Violet's blood as it flowed around me in the back of our escape van; her excitement at a reunion with her daughter that would never come to fruition.

No. I wouldn't take the easy option here. I was going to do what was right and I was going to buy humanity a freedom they hadn't had from the moment they landed on Earth Two.

"I'm sorry," my words are genuine but firm. "This isn't your fault," I reassure him.

his words. He knows this is an argument he can't win and I suddenly miss the brash boy who had first walked into the shack in Nomad's land. He might have been full of anger but it was a spark I respected, in this moment he seemed defeated and broken. Like all the risks he'd taken had been worthless and I suppose, in a way, they had been.

"You saved me from the State. Now I'm going to save everyone else."

I look at him, hoping he understands the meaning behind my words. He's one of three people who know that we have a cure. I don't trust the woman who hasn't taken her eyes off me. She may be the reason I'm still here rather than on my way to the Government's court but this secret was too big to share with her. Even though I was certain she wasn't a State Agent I couldn't be certain she wasn't an Anarchist. And I didn't want my mother to know about the cure until it was too late. She was as bad as the State when it came to the disease and the mutations it promised. She wanted her own army even if her battle was more righteous than greedy. I couldn't let her rip more families apart as she had mine just to achieve her aims.

The boy nods at me and takes a step back. He's understood why I have to leave, why I don't have the time to stay hidden from our enemies. Despite his young years, he knows that what I have to do is bigger than staying undercover. It's what I've told myself repeatedly since I made my decision. The end game is bigger than the pieces I have to move in order to

pride had stopped me. The amount of friendly faces that were now willing to help me was astounding. Whether it was a subtle nod to a hiding place when agents were near or a large shadow to shelter behind when the security cameras pointed my way - every small act by one of her allies made my journey that much easier.

A small voice in the back of my mind wondered why she hadn't arranged for this as soon as I returned to the Settlement - surely Carla would have made her aware of the fact I'd crossed the border, under the guise of visiting Ryle.

Ryle. Of course, that's why she hadn't pulled out all the stops for me until now. She was concerned that I would endanger Ryle. That I would tilt whatever plan they were working on with my presence. Maybe she was even worried that in my quest to seek revenge on the State I'd kill her nephew. I was long past being angry at Ryle though. And even when I had been mad at him I never would have hurt him.

If I was being honest with myself, I'd been more hurt than angry anyway. I thought we trusted each other. I cared about him but in the end, it turned out he'd been keeping secrets from me. Secrets that could have saved me a lot of heartache. But that was done now. That was in the past. The only way I'd even consider hurting Ryle now was if he were to try and stop me from distributing the cure. I knew that wasn't a possibility. That man was a kind soul. He wanted to save him though, his ego would swell and he'd make outlandish promises that would disappear in the wind. All he wanted was for our relationship to move back to a friendlier ground. I would be lying if I didn't admit that I also knew he'd like it to be more than that. Everyone gets one great love in their life and Leo was mine. Is mine. Ryle can never replace that.

With Leo's face at the forefront of my mind, I approach the guard hut at the crossing. This time round it's manned by two Agents, as opposed to the usual part-time guards. Clearly, they've been called in because of the captive on the loose. I can see their weapons leaning against their seats, itching to be fired. I slow my pace and watch from a distance as they scan everybody's ID chips, shining a torch into their face to highlight their features.

Shit. I had no idea whose face was on my ID chip but I was certain I would bear no resemblance to them. In the same way, I was certain that the agents would now have an up-to-date description or CCTV shot of me, rendering any changes I made to my appearance over the last two years pointless.

As I'm considering my options, two men barge past me roughly, causing my backpack to slip from my shoulders onto the floor. I curse at them under my breath and kneel to pick it up, glancing inside at the contents to make sure none of the test tubes have broken, thankfully they are all still in one piece.

They were causing such a scene that people in the queue for the crossing, left their position and gathered around the two fighters, chanting and riling them up.

"Now."

Carla placed a hand under my arm and helped me to my feet. She smiled at me and walked away. To anybody watching, she was a stranger showing me kindness. I didn't have the time to thank her as I watched the agents leave their station to break up the fight. It was only growing in volume and violence with each passing minute. The post was unmanned. This was my chance to cross the border without being caught.

My feet were quick and I ducked under the gate, feeling an intense sense of relief as my shoes touched the ground in Nomad's land. I was one step closer to doing the right thing and it was all thanks to Bailey. Just as quickly as the distraction had begun the two men stopped fighting, the crowd dispersed with an audible groan and the agents picked their way back up the path toward the hut. Not wanting to stick around to see how long my luck lasted, I made my way deeper into Nomad's land, heading towards a building I'd once sworn never to set foot in.

I've only seen photos or video footage of the treatment centre. Sometimes the images were grainy, other times they were in HD. It all depended on the story the media wanted to spin and whether they wanted to paint my mother as something from a horror film or someone who disregarded science. More often than not she'd be a wild woman, a dangerous beast, something so-called accident. The night she sent her husband to kill mine.

Jack. Her husband. My so-called stepfather. I try to place a pin in my feelings toward him as I pick through the rusted and desolate structure. When his finger pulled that trigger, he ripped my happily ever after apart. He changed my life forever and ruined my son's safe home.

On my wedding day to Ryle, when I realised that it had been Jack at the end of the sniper's rifle, I'd acted impulsively. Full of hate and resentment I'd hoped to cave his head in with a wine bottle and perhaps if my aim had been a little firmer, or his arms a little weaker, I might have succeeded. If I had killed him then I certainly wouldn't be living with the regret of that decision now. I'd never wanted to hurt anyone more in my life than I'd wanted to hurt him in that moment, as though spilling his blood would erase my grief. It wouldn't have though. Grief is, unfortunately, something you have to learn to live with and work through.

A rusted bookshelf clung to one of the few remaining walls and I kept one hand upon it for balance as I picked my way across burnt carpet tiles. My mother really had done a number on this place. I'd watched the CCTV footage countless times throughout my life, hoping for a moment when she'd look full of regret for her actions. It never came. My mother had no regrets, she'd told the judge as much. I never imagined how physically being in this building would affect me though. I could almost hear her screams echoing in the but I know it's true.

Why else would she throw her life away to destroy this building and those who worked in it? That's the sort of behaviour you only undertake for true love. That's the kind of revenge that only losing the other half of your soul can cause. I should know. I'd felt it in the storage room when I attacked Jack. The blind rage when confronted by those that had hurt the one you love most.

Mum had not tried to flee from the scene of her crime, she'd chosen instead to sit nearby and watch the flames take hold of the building. She'd barricaded any doors or windows before she entered so that any survivors of the onslaught she'd organised would die before help could reach them. It was a particularly twisted bit of forward planning and the final nail in the coffin when it came to her conviction. An insane person wouldn't have been that logical in the moment, they wouldn't have conceived of such a plan to ensure maximum death.

When she saw the State Agents arriving, she came home to me and asked me to run away with her. I can still remember the look on her face and the smell of her skin as she pleaded with me to pack a backpack and blindly follow her. I'd refused. She'd left without turning back to double-check my answer. Maybe things would have been different if I'd gone with her, perhaps she would have tried harder to stay out of prison. Perhaps she would have calmed down and become the mother I truly loved.

happened. She lost her happily ever after and I know she would never have wanted me to live through the same. The mother I had grown up with died in the treatment centre that night along with her many victims. I've been grieving for her ever since.

I find a couple of loose stones in one of the remaining walls and with a quick look around me pull them out. I open my backpack, pull out the vials of the cure, and place them inside. Sending a silent prayer up to Leo and Violet to keep the cure safe, I place the stones back in their place and take a step away to survey my work. Thankfully the building is in such a state of disarray they don't stand out as having been moved or even being loose. I can't risk Bailey getting her hands on the cure or even becoming aware of its existence. She's as tricky as my mother and I wasn't sure what her view on the mutations was and whether she'd want to stop them.

"Hello agapi mou," comes a voice I've both longed for and dreaded hearing again.

I keep my eyes stubbornly fixed on my feet as I try to control my emotions. So, Bailey had sent my mother to meet with me, rather than having the balls to face me herself. At least Bailey's behaviour is never surprising. She never gets her hands dirty.

I haven't spoken to my mother in years and I've dreamt of this moment countless times since I found she was the reason Leo was put to death. Yet every exchange I've fantasised about disappears from my

But I, in some sick way, still love her. There's still a part of me that's linked to her, that needs her. At least for now.

"Hello, mother."

I finally pull my gaze from the floor and stare into her dark brown eyes. Eyes that used to hold my entire universe within their depths. Eyes that I know I'll close forever.

hovering at her side longing to reach for me. I take a
step back and fix her with a dispassionate gaze. Her hair
is as wild as ever but it seems to have lost its shine.
She's not physically as magnetic as she used to be. It's as
though her personality has fractured and her skin
weighs beneath it.

In different circumstances, I might feel pity
towards the woman who brought me into the world but
it feels like karma has finally come for her and I can't
say I blame it. Hell, I've spent many nights begging it to.

"Bailey's messenger now are you?"

"When I heard you asked to meet with her, I
offered to step in."

Her voice is softer than I remember. I guess my
memories had been clouded by many nightmares of her
scream as we drove into the lake. Is this the voice she'd
used when I was a child and had a question? Part of me
wanted to dredge up that memory to see if that was the
case but my resentment wouldn't allow me.

"Demanded more likely."

"Paige, let me explain-"

I can't let her lead this conversation just as she had
most others in our lifetime. She doesn't deserve that.
She doesn't get to have that anymore.

Without realising it, my hand has found its way
around a large rock, my fingers finding comfort in its
grooves and strengths. When did I stop thinking of her
as Di, my enemy? When did I start remembering her as
my mother again? It wasn't right. I should feel nothing

Despite her advancing years, she's still a physically powerful woman. If she wanted to wrestle the rock from me I wouldn't stand a chance. Something in her expression told me she wouldn't though, that she would accept her fate. My knuckles constrict as I tighten my grip on the rock. I could very easily find it within myself to bring it crashing down upon her skull. I wondered if her bones were as strong as Jack's or whether this attack to the head would be more successful.

When would I stop the blows? When I saw blood? Bone? Brain? What would feel enough to absolve her of the wrongs she has forced upon me? What was Leo's life worth? Violet's? Regina's? If she'd never attacked our car who's to say how our story would have gone? The three of us could be living a quiet life in Nomad's land with Violet and Ada. Perhaps everything would have happened exactly as it did. My mother took that choice out of fate's hand though when she decided, once again, that her morals and her fight for justice were worth more than her daughter.

She was still watching me, painfully aware that she stood in front of a powder keg of her own creation. Isn't this what she'd always wanted? To raise a woman who fought for what she believed to be right? To raise a daughter who could stand up to all the evil in her world? I imagine taking the steps towards her, bringing the rock down and through her head. I'm watching her face twist and contort in pain until it emptied of emotion and her eyes grew dull. I can't say it's an image that brings me wedding. That his name was on the list of lives I'd taken.

She deserved to lose another life partner, something I never thought I'd say about anyone. My mother shakes her head and goes to talk again, apologies and explanations on the tip of her tongue. I interrupt her before she can start weaving her words around me.

"Tell me, what would hurt more, to lose a husband or to lose a daughter?" I make sure to let my voice quiver on the word daughter, as though I'm of fragile mind and likely to cause myself harm.

"I-"

"Relax. I'm not going anywhere."

I try to chuckle light-heartedly but it sounds hollow and manic. Her hand is still hovering at her side, desperate for a kind touch. Desperate for that connection between parent and child. A desperation I was all too familiar with, thanks to her.

I've already wasted too much time on this back and forth between us, enjoying her feelings of displacement. Every moment wasted another life could be lost. I had to stop being selfish and start moving forward with my plan.

Taking a deep breath I explain, "I don't want to talk about it. Not yet. If this is going to work, and it has to, you are my colleague. Nothing else."

My voice is open and honest and I hope she can tell it's genuine. As much as it pains me, I need her to succeed, anything after that is yet to be decided.

"Can you agree to these terms?"

I am in control. For the first time in our relationship, I am the one in control, the one manipulating the situation for my benefit. She must feel so misplaced. Good. She should feel how I felt countless times growing up - unheard. Spoken over. Controlled. She always loved me, I have always said that. She just loved me more when I agreed with her.

Years ago my mother would have dealt with my insolence by walking away, punishing me by withholding her presence until eventually, we reached an uneasy compromise. Now, if she walked away, she risked losing me forever. Something that until this moment, until I saw the thought process flick across her face, I would have assumed, meant very little to her. She had chosen to go to prison. Chosen to be a martyr. Chosen to raise the rebellion rather than me. You can love someone and not value them - those feelings are not mutually interlinked. My mother loved me as if I were the most precious thing in the entire universe. But she never valued me. Never trusted me. Never thought she might truly lose me. Always counted on our love for each other to get us through anything.

Now the woman in front of me, whom I barely recognise, nods once to show her compliance to my request. She believes the time for words and forgiveness will come, once this task is complete. She's wrong but I'm not about to tell her that.

"What's the plan?" She asks in a businesslike tone. Clipped and emotionless. Ready to follow my orders.

cried out at the shadow she became in that moment and
it took a lot of self-control to not reach out to her with
a kind smile and a hug of reassurance. She's my mother.
I love her.

"We're going to stop the Téssera."

I know she won't disagree with my mission, she's
spent my whole life trying to destroy the State and the
people who stood behind the curtains.

"How?"

She's not a stupid woman. She knows the answer to
her question. She just wants to know if her only child is
on the same page. She needs to know how far I am
willing to go to right this wrong and create a safer world
for everyone in the Settlement.

"How do you think?"

She will not lead this conversation. I will be the one
asking the questions. She does not get to control this
situation or our relationship. Not after everything she
has caused me to lose. She's my mother. I hate her.

"There's only one way to stop things permanently."

She gestures at the building, or the skeleton of the
building around us.

"You burn it to the ground."

I smile at her for the first time since she arrived but
it's not the smile of a daughter pleased to see her
mother. It's the smile of a crusader who's met her army.

"Thankfully I know where to light the fuse."

there was no other word for the sound of derision that came from her mouth at my declaration. Despite the eggshells being crushed beneath our feet, her ego couldn't begin to believe her daughter had succeeded where she'd failed. She wouldn't believe that I knew how to destroy the Téssera.

"Nobody knows who they are, Paige."

Parents have a particular tone that they use on their children when they're trying to show them they love them whilst patronising them. The kind of tone that sets their adult child's skin on fire and causes a visceral reaction. I'm a pre-teen again, desperate for the world to understand and listen to me. Hormonally charged passion at the perceived insult in her tone makes me want to stamp my feet and swear. That's not logical though, and if I start behaving emotionally right now, then there won't be much hope for the two of us to walk out of this building alive.

"It's not your fault my darling, I have made the same mistake myself before."

How kind of her to reassure me that I am not a failure. If she's trying to shoot me a comforting smile, then her face is failing spectacularly. All I can see on her features is disappointment in my wild belief in myself. Of course, I could never achieve what she'd always failed at. She would always be the adult in our relationship and adults were never wrong.

"Did you know Regina's father was one of the original members?" I ask.

"Did Leo...?"

She asks her question without filling in the blanks. She wants to know if my husband, the man she had killed, had been a part of the cruellest collection of humans amongst us. His name was on her lips. She has no right to speak his name.

"How dare you..."

Careful Paige, tread carefully. You can't become emotional. She's a colleague, not your mother. I hold my angry tears back and take a deep breath.

"No. He did not." I reply.

Detaching myself from the memory of my good and kind husband, I revert back to business. Leo is just a name. It's just a word. I have to pretend that hearing it in her voice doesn't break my heart all over again.

I need something from her, therefore I must appeal to her. Get her on my side. Be the daughter she raised, and forget the losses you have faced because of her actions. The picture is bigger than your grief right now.

"Right. Of course."

There is no doubt upon her face, that she has taken my words to be true. As she should.

"I can't believe Gina never told me" she spoke to herself, disappointed that her childhood friendship with my mother-in-law wasn't quite as strong as she believed.

"I'm not sure what my current husband's plans are for his inheritance though. His father is the member who runs the President's office."

with the man. Paige Grima was never a name I sought
for myself and it was one I was looking forward to
losing, as soon as possible.

"Well I never…" she smiled to herself and shook
her head as a memory flitted across her face.

God, I hope she hasn't slept with my father-in-law.

"But he seems so…dull." She says.

It might be hard to believe but my mother didn't
think of that word as an insult. At least not in the way I
might. What she means when she says dull, is normal.
Anton seems so normal. She doesn't believe in a world
full of big personalities like hers that would lead to all
sorts of drama that could easily be avoided. She believes
her type of eccentricities, as she calls them, should be an
anomaly and not the norm. So being dull is what 90% of
the population should be and she wasn't wrong in her
surface assessment of Anton, as being part of the
majority.

On the surface, Anton was as interesting as a rusty
penny. That's where the beauty of his deception shines
though. He's the best dentist in the Settlement, with a
waiting list just about everyone has been on. When he
isn't poking around in people's mouths he can be found
at the local library, picking up a new recipe book or
taking part in one of the many neighbourhood meetings
for his street. He's had five tickets from the State for
various small-time offences, like most of us, and he
enjoys gardening when he is able.

He is everything a good, compliant, and normal
member of our civilisation should be. There is nothing

paranoid person I knew.

"He ordered the President's death." I say.

I share this titbit with her so she understands just how high up in the organisation Anton sits. There may only be four of them but as with any organisation, there would be a hierarchy behind the scenes and I was about to gamble everything on Anton being a vital cog in the machine.

"He organised my relationship with Ryle."

Her eyebrows raise at my use of the word relationship but she doesn't pass comment.

"I was lined up to be the perfect First Lady. It would have been a lovely story."

"If only you hadn't killed the assistant."

She makes no mention of my assault on Jack, a wise move. How did she know that Paul's death had caused the tape to leak? Bailey. Of course. If Ryle had known then of course Bailey had known which meant my mother knew. I hadn't realised the two former allies were still in contact. I assumed they'd cut ties after the attack on the centre we stood in.

"Leave it with me." She turns to leave, ready to send her minions out to gather the intelligence we need.

"It was good to see you."

I can't bring myself to return her pleasantries so I settle for a half-hearted grunt, a way to acknowledge her words without returning the sentiment. Listening to her retreating footsteps I feel all manner of emotions and ages. I'm a child watching her mother walk away from her after her decision to stay was respected. I'm a let them overtake me.

I pull my knees up into my chest as I sit on the floor, lay my arms across them, and rest my head in the crook of my elbow. In for four. Out for eight. In for four. Out for eight. I know it would be easier to expand my chest fully if I weren't hunched over myself but right now my need to feel hidden is greater than my need to calm my anxiety.

This was all too much.

I shouldn't have taken on so much at the same time. My brain can't cope. I'm plotting against Ryle's father. I've just met my mother for the first time since discovering she killed my husband. I'm sat in a building I swore never to step foot in, the building that robbed me of my childhood. I don't know how much longer I can function with all the conflicting thoughts swirling around inside of me. I just want to lie down and sleep. I feel as though I haven't rested since our safe house got attacked.

Sleep would be so beneficial right now. I was fairly certain I'd be protected if I were to indulge. My mother and Bailey would be certain to have guards posted nearby, in case of spies. Truth be told though, right now I was afraid to fall asleep. Afraid of what my subconscious mind might want to sift through. Would it be an evening long ago with Violet and Leo for company? Or would it be the memory of all the people we lost in our quest for the cure? Perhaps it would be the sound of my mother's scream on repeat as she sent would Ryle take the news?

I knew that father and son had a very complicated relationship. Ryle carried a lot of anger towards his father for the way he was prioritised over the life of his mother. She'd taken her last breath long before Ryle took his first. He'd told me it felt as though his father had sentenced him to live life as a murderer before he'd even taken his first breath. What kind of legacy was that for a child? But Anton was still his father. There would still be an inexplicable biological bond between them, whether or not Ryle wanted there to be.

At least my mother had loved me. In her good moments, she had made me the centre of her world. I had never worried that I was a burden or that I should be seen and not heard. But Ryle had. Maybe that would make his father's death easier because the love my mother had for me, and I for her, definitely muddied the waters around what I knew I eventually had to do. If anyone else had broken my family so fatally I wouldn't hesitate to rain down revenge upon them. But she wasn't anyone. She was my mother. I looked up to her. I learned from her. I longed for her. Could I push past all of that and hurt her?

I wish I'd killed Jack at the wedding, then on some level, I'd at least feel we were even right now. But no, the resilient bastard had to survive. He survived injuries that would have killed a lesser man and boy was he living pretty on that story. Not literally, of course, his pleasing facial features hadn't survived the blows from the wine bottle. Neither had his easygoing charm. Jack,

"Paige?"

My mother's voice is calling me back to the conscious world and I have to fight the urge to strangle it from her throat. Dreams can have that effect on you, sometimes they feel more real than reality.

"Paige?"

I can't reply to her yet. I have to steady my breathing or else I'll be lost to a full anxiety attack. Focus on something you can see. Something you can hear. Something you can touch. Breathe in for four counts, out for eight. It was just a dream. Just a bad dream.

her. I'm pleasantly surprised as to how much she is respecting my boundaries at the moment.

"What have you found out?" My voice is croaky, as everyone tends to be after a night of sleep with nothing to drink.

Without offering she pushes a flask and a wrapped-up bundle towards me. I reach out and feel the warm metal of the flask. Unscrewing the lid slightly, the earthy aroma of coffee hits my nose and I'm practically salivating. I tentatively take a sip and enjoy the light-burning sensation on my tongue. Reaching out towards the bundle, I pull it towards me. The two slices of bread are still warm and doughy and inside is some kind of cheese and meat, my stomach rumbles loudly in gratitude.

"Thanks, Mum." I can't help the words as they tumble out and instantly regret them. She isn't my mum today. She's my colleague.

There's a slight tilt of her lips upwards in response to my words but she has the good grace not to verbally acknowledge them. She can respect my rules, even if I can't.

"You eat and I'll tell you what I know," she offers. I'm so famished I barely let her finish her sentence before I tuck in.

childhood home, after what he put me through, but I guess it's a form of Stockholm syndrome. This house is my childhood home. Keeper of my best memories as well as my worst. I could walk down the hallways and remember birthday parties, carefully orchestrated for publicity of course, but also barrels of fun for a boy who was essentially a shut-in. Or whilst standing in the kitchen, I would remember feeling like an adult for the first time as Aunt Bailey made me a hot chocolate to go alongside her coffee. We sat together at the counter, sharing secrets and she laughed when the cream covered my nose. So you see, as much as I'm also haunted by the memories of a cold and distant father, I'm also comforted by the warmth and love I managed to find within these walls.

I made my way downstairs to the pantry and picked through the shelves until I found some coffee granules and pastries that caught my eye. My father would have insisted I let the chef take care of my breakfast but I always fed myself when I lived here and I wasn't about to change old habits now. In the staff kitchen, I found the microwave and the old French press that had once sat in pride of place in the family kitchen. I guess once it had served its purpose, father had it replaced. The fact he couldn't do that with me caused him no end of aggravation.

A microwave was another item on his list that wasn't allowed in the main house. They were unsightly things, the tools of the bored and stupid. Nothing pride, feeling like I'd got one over on him. I had really thought I was finally free. The naivety of youth. He'd cut my credit cards off for a week after that purchase and I'd made do living off instant noodles, brought with my meagre salary from waiting tables. He had been furious at first when I'd told him that was my plan to pay my rent. But of course, in the end, it had played perfectly into his story of the down-to-earth politician. I'd worked 'normal' jobs just like each of the voters. I was one of them and it was always easy to vote for one of your own. Who better to look after your interests than someone who has actually lived your life and knows first-hand the problems you face, day in and day out?

I waited tables for a year before starting my first campaign for junior mayor of Zone One. The easiest zone to win over, according to my campaign manager and one in which my youth would go in my favour. It also helped that the restaurant I had worked in for a year was in that particular zone. One of the most popular with the locals and therefore the people who voted with their feet when Election Day came. I spent twelve months charming them all each time they visited, as well as actually learning from them. I felt it was important to actually learn from this experience, to become the normal man they perceived me to be. I didn't want to be as false as my father and without his knowledge, I forged friendships, genuine friendships with some patrons. People who spent their time trying line to help uphold the idea that love is love, no matter what my father's government says. I started making weekly donations to the cause, out of my cash tips, passing it under the table to the patron who worked directly with the cause. He assured me that every penny was spent on medical supplies to aid insemination for desperate people and I finished every shift with a sense of fulfilment when I saw him walk out of the restaurant, with my envelope. I was helping to make a difference. And my father truly had no idea.

These days I'm unable to make cash donations outright. My money is monitored by many faceless accountants. All of whom ultimately report back to my father. Instead, once a week, I go back to the restaurant I'd worked in and leave an incredibly healthy tip after each of my meals. Father asked me once why I insisted on this routine and I reminded him it kept me grounded in the eyes of the public. I was compliant in his plan for my career and it was a stroke of genius to show that I didn't consider myself to have outgrown my roots.

He brought into my lie because of course he did. It fed into his ego. It made him believe he'd raised a good and malleable son. That we were on the same page about my future and the future of the Settlement. But we weren't. A hundred tiny rebellions had happened underneath his nose since I became an adult and they were only going to increase in volume now I was President.

By seeing through his plan to its final stage, he'd actually ensured its destruction. I smiled to myself again main house and listen out for the sounds of my father's morning routine. I hear the rustling of a newspaper and know he's nearby. Peering round the corner of the door frame into the formal dining room I take a moment to truly look at him. He's aged a lot in the last few years, no longer the sprightly man I used to look up to. His posture isn't quite as straight as normal either. His shoulders are hunched over slightly as he reads the day's headlines. Five years ago I would have placed money on the position of my father's shoulders always being upright. The way a man held himself was important, it was the first impression the world took of him.

"Are you just going to stand there?" My father asked, not raising his eyes from the paper in front of him.

I shuffled into the room like a naughty schoolboy, all too prepared for the lecture he was about to impart to me.

"That was a smart move yesterday."

He almost sounded impressed with my actions as he gestured to the seat opposite him. I sat down and tried not to roll my eyes as he slid a plate towards me for my pastry. Heaven forbid I spill crumbs in the formal dining room.

"I'm glad you enjoyed it." I make a show of leaning into the middle of the table to pick out a coaster for my mug. Might as well play at being civil, if that's what he wanted.

"My colleagues weren't quite as impressed."

I shrug nonchalantly, here comes the lecture.

happening." He paused, waiting for a response.

"Thank you, father." I take a sip from my coffee to swallow the resentment those words brought up from my stomach. I didn't care that the Téssera weren't impressed with my actions. I wasn't stupid. I knew I was quickly becoming more of a problem than a solution. All I cared about was whether Paige had avoided capture, but I couldn't very well ask my father directly. I couldn't let him know quite how much I cared.

"Now, we won't be having another outburst like that again, will we?" The question is rhetorical. And patronising. If he counted that as an outburst what would he make of the thoughts swirling in my head? How would he react to the grand changes I wanted to make to the political landscape of the Settlement? Would he step in to protect me from his colleague's wrath or would he, once again, choose his beliefs and career over family? The small boy that still lived in my heart desperately hoped that this time it would be different. That this time my father would choose his family's well-being over himself. But the man I'd grown into knew better than that.

He'd loved my mother that I knew for certain. He lived within the mausoleum of her influence and dreams by keeping their house exactly the same as she left it. And yet, he'd still chosen his beliefs in the Repopulation Act over her life. Bailey told me he had to leave the room as my mother took her last unassisted breaths. After that, she was hooked up to life support so I could continue growing to term. Guilt had prevented him allowed the two of them to grow old happily together. But he didn't. He left the room and went back to his office to continue his list of correspondence for the week. It was Bailey who held her hand as she slipped from this life to the next. Bailey who checked on her every day, marvelling at how her stomach continued to grow despite her soul being in the ether. Bailey who held me when I was first born wept over the sacrifice her sister had been forced to make.

When I thought of all that I knew, my self-righteous rage grew. If he thought that announcement was an outburst, he had another thing coming.

"No sir." I bow my head slightly and avoid his gaze. Even after all these years, there was still a tiny part of me that wanted his approval, a part of me that despised lying to him.

"Good. Now, I've booked us a table for dinner tonight at the Waterfall. I trust you will be able to join me?" He's probably already had my diary cleared.

"No, sir." The shock on his face is noticeable as he puts the paper on the table.

"I believe you are free,"

"Your sources are incorrect." Only now can I meet his eye.

Now those years of resentment are bubbling up through me again. I didn't have time to indulge him in a father and son photo opportunity which is all it would be. We'd be photographed turning up at the restaurant talking animatedly whilst in the presence of the media and then when we were alone we'd eat in awkward

down on the table, wiping my mouth with the napkin to
the left of the plate. Pushing my chair back, I make to
stand only to find my father mirroring my movement.
Was he intending to try and stop me from leaving? Did
he really believe he stood a chance against me in a
physical altercation? I was going to walk out of this
room and away from the house and nobody was going
to stop me. I had to make it back to my office so I
could request a debrief on Paige's movements. That's
what any President would do.

"Where are you going?"

"Back to the office. I'm sure I have a lot of
catching up to do." He takes a step towards me as I pass
him, but instead of trying to stop me he holds out his
hand and shakes mine.

"You'll be a fine President son, once you've got
your house in order."

I didn't understand the context of his words at first
but could guess as to who he was referring to. Paige.
She was what he wanted me to get in order. She was
what was preventing me from being a fine President.

The good President he had raised. Paige has
nothing to do with my rebellion, she'd be a suitable
partner for it but she is not the cause of it. My father
himself is the cause of it. His distinct lack of empathy
for others is why I'm so determined to help them. If
only he truly knew the kind of President he'd raised.

the restaurant by the waterfall. In fact, he had the table booked behind the waterfall; the very table Leo and I had booked for our anniversary night. The reservation we never made it to.

I'm sure Anton didn't have to ask a friend to call in a favour to secure it. He probably had his own direct hotline to the owner for such occasions. A thunderstorm was forecast to start later this evening, one of the biggest ones of the year so far. No wonder he'd chosen tonight to take advantage of his social standing. The lake at the bottom of the waterfall would be a sizzling ballet of nature as the boiling raindrops met their icy depths. The purple lightning strikes would highlight the rising steam resulting in the kind of natural theatre we don't often get to witness.

I wondered if Anton would join the other patrons after his meal and dip his feet in the lake once the clouds had cleared, enjoying one of the rare times the lake wasn't ice cold. I doubted it. He probably thought such acts trivial. Something the lower echelons of society indulged in. He'd probably enjoy watching them all throw their heads back in laughter as the fish tickled the soles of their feet. Maybe he'd be secretly hoping for one of them to nip at somebody's skin, the yelps of pain would be music to his ears.

I had never met the man, he hadn't been able to make it to our wedding - citing a dental emergency of all things. It's something Ryle had said he was pleased about. He didn't want to subject me to his dad's

She's playing the part of the good soldier, leaving responsibility and decisions up to me, lest I accuse her of trying to usurp this mission. I know she doesn't mean it though, she's just biding her time, waiting for an opening where she can win my forgiveness.

"If the table is booked for five, then we should be there for half past. Let him settle in, get comfortable. Then we strike."

A plan is formulated in my mind. A risky one. One that involves putting myself directly in the firing line. But if we succeed, if we can cut off one hand of the Téssera, then we will have taken a step toward a better world for Franklin and Ada. I owed that to them. It's what Violet and Leo would want from me, to make the world a safer place for our children.

"Perfect. I will be back to collect you."

"Could you bring some more coffee?" I mildly plead.

She smiles and nods her head in response to my request, clearly pleased that our interactions are already growing friendlier and less volatile. I watch her leave with a sense of detachment. I'm getting better at seeing her as a colleague rather than as my mum.

Whilst she's gone, I busy myself by checking, and then rechecking, on the cure's hiding place. As though it might grow legs and walk away on its own volition. That would be useful. Then it could go and distribute itself whilst I took care of the Anton problem. Two birds with one stone. Unfortunately, I don't live in a fantasy world where test tubes grow legs and fulfil their purpose somehow I lose them? No. They are safer waiting here for me to return.

True to her word my mother arrives back at the treatment centre, just before five, with another flask of piping hot coffee.

"You aren't going to like my plan, but it is the best one." She fixes me with a steely gaze that tells me her next words will be a good-natured lie.

"Whatever you need."

I nod at her and without any more words we walk, matching our pace as we always used to, out of the treatment centre and onto the next chapter of our story. Nobody pays us a second glance as we pick our way through Nomad's land towards the Waterfall, which is surprising, given we are two of the State's most wanted fugitives. It's either a sign of my mother's reach or of the general apathy in Nomad's land towards the State and its rules. Whichever it was, I was grateful for it. I needed the peace to prepare myself for what was to come. The sound of the waterfall crashing into the lake hit our ears long before we saw the restaurant appear.

When I was a child, I'd dreamt of a goddess that lived atop the waterfall. Keeping a watchful eye over the residents of Nomad's land, ensuring our safety at all times. She was a kind being. Not vengeful and full of self-righteous rules like some of the Gods' people prayed to. Other people didn't know of her existence and therefore, the idea of her hadn't been corrupted by people trying to use her as a way to achieve their own aims and control. As I watched the water cascading

As we approach the side entrance to the restaurant, I nod at my mother. I notice the hesitation on her features, she doesn't want to leave me to do this step on my own. She wants to stay by my side and keep me safe. But splitting up is the greatest chance we have at success and thankfully, I don't need to remind her of that. She never sways far from her righteous cause. After a beat, she returns my nod and breaks away from my side, picking her way up the steps that lead to the top of the waterfall.

For those dining behind the water, a car is supplied by the restaurant in order to safely traffic them through the freezing and intensely powerful flow. Up ahead, I can see one returning down the side of the mountain. Anton must have sent it away for the night. He'd arrived on time as we presumed. As it approaches, I can make out two figures riding in its seats. His security no doubt.

Turning my chest towards the staff entrance, I make a show of holding my empty hand over the scanner as though I'm trying to clock in for my shift. The security guards pay me no mind as the car slows and reaches its parking space, just behind me to the left. I listen to their conversation as they make their way around to the front of the restaurant, I had hoped they'd be stationed a little further away but clearly, the allure of the upcoming weather was too much for them to miss. I wondered if they were able to claim the cost of the meal on their expenses. I hope not.

I took a deep breath and waited until I heard the front door close before I moved again making my way

on its service mode so anyone could access it. It had
been on that mode all day, therefore the activation
couldn't be traced to this exact time or journey.

I don't duck down into the seat as it makes it way
up the waterfall. There is no need to hide my presence.
The clouds in the sky are forming. Anyone sensible
would be sheltering in place and anyone less than
sensible was not somebody I had to concern myself
with. Nobody believes the words of the insane anyway.
Even though I know I'm completely safe I still flinch at
the sound of the waterfall hitting the car. It roars
through the metal shell all around me, causing creaks
and groans from the vehicle that raise my heart rate.
Then, just as suddenly as it starts, it stops and I'm
through.

I push against the ceiling panel as instructed by my
mother and find a button just as she described, one tiny
tap, and the car pulls to a stop before reaching the table
where Anton will be dining. The sound of the car
chundering through the water would have no doubt
caught his attention but he was so self-absorbed he
would assume it was the waiting staff with his first
course. I made the rest of the journey towards him on
foot, choosing my steps carefully to make as little noise
as possible.

I passed the emergency ladder on my way. It
follows the path of the waterfall up to its peak, where a
short tunnel then transports you to the top of the
mountain. It hasn't been used since it was first built.
Technology barely failed since we arrived on Earth

you to my invented goddess of the waterfall. He finally
hears my footsteps and calls out to me,

"Another glass of Merlot!"

No pleases or thank yous. He doesn't need to
waste those words on service staff. I wonder who, a
man of his stature, deems his manners worthy of. I will
teach my son the same thing I was taught - manners
cost nothing and should be shared with everyone. Be
kind to everyone you meet on your way up in life as you
never know who you will meet on your way down.
That's what Grandpa Joe always used to say. Be wary of
punching down. Nobody stays at the top forever. Not
even Anton.

"Of course sir" I reply moving towards him.

This is the moment I have to be most careful of. I
need him to recognise me but I have to be aware that he
has cutlery near his hands. The last thing I need is for
him to be quicker with the steak knife than I am on my
feet.

Just as I suspected, he doesn't look up at me. It
would be so easy to despatch him here. No one would
know until the restaurant realised he hadn't called
through for his second course but that wasn't the plan.

Despite what I did to Paul and the man in grey,
killing is not in my nature. Those kills were almost self-
defence. A way to protect myself from men who had
spent our entire time together delighting in being cruel
to me. This was different. I couldn't bring myself to spill
my father-in-law's blood. That's the truth of it. I didn't
want Ryle to look at me and see his father's death

owner's business would be under intense scrutiny for months if the murder happened here. The State would close the restaurant for as long as they could, perhaps permanently, as punishment for letting the blood of the Téssera run within its walls. I wouldn't let anyone else take the wrath for what we were here to do.

It was to be clear that this was an isolated incident. Just an Anarchist and a terrorist working in tandem, taking advantage of Anton's slip in protection. If he hadn't sent his security away then I wouldn't be standing inches from him right now.

"I believe you've been waiting for me?"

Finally, he looks up at me and for a moment he doesn't know who I am. I watch realisation dawn on him. After all, he would have seen the images of me from the CCTV in the Zones earlier in the day. What a confident fool he was to dine alone in such a secluded place knowing I was nearby and on the loose. His ego was his downfall.

He reaches out one hand towards me whilst pressing the intercom on the table with his other.

"Send security. NOW" he bellows as I step away from his grasp.

Standing up, I notice that he's just a touch shorter than his son, that must wind him up no end. I wonder how he felt on the day Ryle outgrew him. The hand from the intercom fumbles around the table until it lands on the steak knife. He doesn't take his eyes off me just in case I'm an apparition that will disappear.

"Run. I always enjoy the chase." The cruel amusement from his lips causes goose bumps to appear on my arm. Thankfully, this breaks the spell he held over me.

Ryle would never speak to anyone in that tone. This is the man who killed his wife just to keep hold of his social standing. Who treated his son as nothing but a political puppet. Who voted to blackmail my husband into creating a disease that tore so many families apart? This man is a monster and he needs to be slain.

escape ladder. He's probably annoyed that I have yet to shriek in fear but there's only so much play-acting I can undertake these days. As my foot hits the first rung, I am surprised to find him only inches behind me, the old man moves with more grace than I'd planned for. I feel the air beneath my ankle move as he takes a swipe at my Achilles tendon. In response, I kick my heel down as hard as I am able, delighting in the grunt he makes as it connects with him.

"I didn't think you'd have this much fight." He chuckles to himself, as I climb further away from him.

He was the same age as my mother but I'd assumed a life of wealth had made him lazy and weak. I hadn't expected him to be nearly as sprightly as her. Listening to his feet jump from rung to rung, I keep expecting the touch of his hand upon my foot again, but it doesn't come. I have to keep going. There is no other choice. The childish part of my brain wants to call out to my mother, to ruin the element of surprise knowing that she will come to my rescue.

"Paige" he calls my name in a sing-song manner. "Paige, security are already on their way. Why don't you let me take you up to greet them? We're family Paige. Come on now, there's no way out for you here."

He's bargaining with me as he continues to pursue me. He wants to be the one to lay hands on me first. To win. That's why he never spoke my name on the intercom. He wants to win the hunt and claim the glory.

thunder that follows causes the ladder to shake. We both pause momentarily as droplets from the waterfall itself are blown upon our backs. The water is so cold I can feel it burning the nape of my neck. I longed for my long protective curls right now but they were gone and my time on the run had at least increased my pain threshold. Nights spent wandering in scalding rain will do that to a person.

I listened as Anton hissed in pain, wondering what part of his body got hit. I realised that it no longer mattered that he was faster than I'd expected. He was no match for the storm nature was about to unleash upon us. Hell, I'd wager he'd even pause at the exit of the tunnel at the sight of the rain. Would his passion to hurt me win over his self-preservation or would he stay sheltered and allow his lackeys the honour of capturing the State's most wanted?

"Keep up old man, it's just a little water," I tease as I resume my climb.

It was dangerous to provoke him I knew but I had to make sure his blood was pumping with nothing but hatred for me by the time we reached the mountaintop. It was the only way to guarantee he'd follow me.

My words had their desired effect and I heard him mutter a curse word before his hands and feet started up again on the steady repetitive motion of climbing the ladder. There was a comfortable distance between us, he was being cautious now. Pausing occasionally whenever a large gust of wind danced too near to prevent himself

He doesn't have the patience for my needling. His confidence has taken a blow. "I can't wait to have you back in the apartment. It won't be as cushy for you this time." He's trying to get into my head, to delay me.

"Sorry, I can't quite hear you from down there you'll have to speak up." I keep my tone light and carefree, the best way to react to someone trying to upset you, is with lightness. They don't know how to manipulate it. "I can see the tunnel!"

"Enjoy the sight, it'll be one of the last you see!"

He isn't attempting to throw the words at me. They are an aside to himself but they carry up to me, nonetheless.

Another crack of thunder signals the start of the downpour; it's impossible to hear anything else over the roar of the water all around us so instead I concentrate on the task at hand. One foot, one hand, one foot, one hand, keep climbing although you feel like your arms may come loose from their sockets.

Before I know it, I'm pulling myself up into the tunnel that leads to the top of the waterfall. Mum will be waiting for me up there - it's up to me to make sure Anton follows despite the heavy downpour. I wait near the exit and watch as he pulls himself up into the tunnel in front of me. I can see little red marks on the back of his hands - that must have been where the splash from the waterfall hit him. Once again I was impressed with his stamina, to keep climbing the ladder for that distance with hand injuries must have been painful but he

"Kind of" I reply before bracing myself and running out of the exit.

The rain beats down on my skin, it's not as hot as I've been imagining or maybe I've just acclimatised. I stand six feet or so away from the exit, refusing to flinch as boiling drops hit my scalp and roll down my face and neck. My body will be covered in welts by the end of this. For a moment my mind wanders to Regina, remembering the burns I put upon her when I tortured her in my lab back at the hospital. Back when I was still searching for the truth about Leo. Back when I still hadn't worked out who to blame. Anton is one reason I lost my husband, my marriage, and my child. I need to hold onto that resentment for the next five minutes.

"Surely you don't think I'm stupid enough to follow you out there?"

"I think you're underestimating my faith in your intellect."

He chuckles at my retort.

"You would have made a good daughter-in-law."

He's being honest in his compliment, I can hear it in his tone. He sounds like Ryle as he speaks, there is a softness to his voice.

"Such a shame you had to ruin it." The venom is back. So that's what this simmers down to. He hates me because I ruined his grand scheme. He hates me because of what I supposedly took from him.

"We spent such a lot of time on you, the time we wasted." He's having to raise his voice now to be heard over the thunder that's punctuating his sentences.

only request. She didn't do her best work in close quarters she stated, knowing that I wanted this to be her peak performance. I tried to ask for more of a reason but she was not forthcoming. I guess she figured that our escape route would be easier if we were on the mountaintop. If we got stuck in the tunnel after we'd dispatched him then we'd have no way out, we'd be sitting ducks. No, she had been right, outside in nature was safer.

"I guess I'll just wait out here until security arrives." Raindrops splash into my mouth as I talk and I feel painful ulcers form on my tongue.

"At least then the reward will go to somebody worthwhile."

I watch as his face contorts, the idea of having to give away some of his wealth for my capture when I am mere feet away is too much for him and he makes his decision. He keeps his eye on me as he pulls out his hanky square, and I watch in fascination as it unfurls in front of me, growing in size. With a showy sigh he holds it out in front of him - the hanky is now a jacket - complete with a hood and from the way it's moving in the wind, it appears it's made from quite sturdy material. Shit. That's a bit of a spanner in the plan.

"Ready or not, here I come." The manic grin is back on his face as he steps out of the tunnel and into the rain. There are no groans of pain this time, he is sheltered from the elements. I am the only one with burning skin. I'm frozen to my spot in fear and I can see it's appealing to him. Before I know it he is standing

"Who are you, Anton?"

"I might ask you the same question, Paige Kearney." He speaks my mother's surname. He knows my story, my secrets, and my heritage.

"Will you ever forgive your mother for having your husband killed?" He sneers at me. "We didn't quite put all the pieces together until you attacked Mr Wright. Then everything about you suddenly made sense."

"I'm glad you found me so interesting." He's pressing down so hard on my arm that it feels as though his fingerprints will imprint on my bones.

"More than interesting my dear. I found you fascinating. It's just a shame my son does too."

He pulls me close to him and for a moment I worry he's going to kiss me. As though he wants to take something of Ryle's as punishment for his son disobeying him.

This time when I try to pull away from him I mean it. I am not an object to be used in a tug-of-war between two men. And I am certainly not going to allow Anton to lay his lips upon me.

"Who are the other members of the Téssera?" I find my voice and hope now that he believes himself to have the upper hand, he'll give me the information I want. We have to know who the other three members are. Dealing with one-quarter of a problem doesn't destroy the problem, it just annoys it.

"That won't matter where you're going."

"Indulge me."

back.

"We know where your son is hiding. Did you really think he'd be safe living with those degenerates?" Another punch comes to my stomach. I shield it slightly with my own arms that are crossed across my torso but the impact is still there. "I'm going to bring them to you and make you watch as the life drains from their eyes."

"I'll kill you." My breathing is laboured through pain but I mean every word. This time he pulls my head up by the hair, I see the outline of my mother walking towards us behind him and smile as he slaps me across the face.

"You're no killer Paige."

"You're right. But my mother is."

He doesn't have time to respond before my mother hits him over the back of the head with a rock. He crumples like a leaf under its impact. She handles him roughly as she pulls the jacket from his body. He's barely able to protest as shock from the blow rushes through his bloodstream. Holding out the jacket towards me she keeps her eyes fixated on the prey at her feet. My arm is limp from the hold he kept on it and I struggle to pull the jacket on. I can tell she wants to help me but she's respecting the lines in the sand I've drawn between us. We are not mother and daughter. We are colleagues bound by a need for death.

"Did he give you any names?" She asks once I finally have the jacket on.

I shake my head and she sighs.

already thinning locks.

"My security will be here shortly."

Mum makes a show of pausing in her movement and raises her head slightly as though she is listening to the world around her. Lightning crackles above us and I see her illuminated as the true warrior she is. She is the goddess of the waterfall I used to dream of. Always trying to keep the Settlement safe.

"I think the storm may have caused some delays, unfortunately." She resumes dragging him until she finally finds a spot she's happy with. By now Anton is shouting out threats, expletives, promises and warnings.

"I can pay you twice what she's offering."

It always comes down to money with people like this. They think they can buy their way out of any situation.

"I'll fund the Anarchists for you." A last ditch attempt to convince her to change sides.

A clever one to give him credit. She does after all, love being the mother to her movement, more than anything else in the world.

My mother drops him to the floor in the largest puddle she can set her eyes upon.

"My daughter is worth more than all the wealth in this world."

She kicks him onto his back and before he or I can react, she plunges a nail through his palm. I wince as he screams out in pain. Maybe I don't have the stomach for this. Then I remember Violet's blood on my hand, all the families the disease and its mutations have ripped from the downpour and he closes his eyes to try and shield his sight.

"Give us the names." She orders, her voice low and ominous. One I've never heard before. My inner child cowers before the stranger she's morphing into. So this was my mother at work. I'd never witnessed it in person. Sure, I'd witnessed first-hand the minor cases of breaking and entering, the manipulation of others, and the everyday rebellions but never had I seen her embrace violence. She was enthralled with it at this moment. That could be my future if I wasn't careful.

The thunder pauses momentarily and in the distance, we can hear a car engine at the bottom of the mountain His security would be here in about ten minutes.

"I'd rather die." He responds to her request with more disdain than I'd expect from a man in his level of pain.

"Oh, you will. But I'd prefer if you gave us the names first."

I'm edging towards this dangerous game of cat and mouse, morbidly curious to watch my mother at play. With more self-control than I think I'd have given his situation, Anton turns his attention towards me.

"If you ever want to see your son again you need to stop this." Once again someone is using my child to control me. I kneel beside him and take in his bleeding hands and burnt skin.

"I don't think you're in any position to be striking deals, do you?"

achieve together." Anton tries another tactic on me, he's appealing to my ego.

"I don't think any achievement will surpass this one." I can't help the smile that is beginning to spread across my face at the sight of him so helpless. This man is one of the most influential on our planet and now he's here, trying to make a deal with me to save his life. As though his life is worth more than the countless he and his colleagues have taken since we settled on Earth Two.

"Are you going to give us the names?"

My mother knows at this point that this is mostly a rhetorical question, Anton will not break and reveal his colleagues. We all know this. She's just waiting for him to confirm it.

"They'll kill me." He sounds scared now as he turns his attention back to her, his face pleading with hers.

"So will we."

She shrugs her shoulders and kneels beside him, opposite me. I want to make eye contact with her, to share in the glory of this moment but she's obsessed with the man lying on the floor before her. I can't say I blame her. This man represents everything she's been fighting against since she was a child. It was his lottery draw that caused the abandonment and death of her birth family. His laws pushed her friends into loveless and often cruel marriages. His treatment centre tortured and killed the love of her life. Anton is at the epicentre of every decision that has changed my mother's life for the worse.

gasps for air. With each gasp new raindrops enter his throat and he groans in agony as they burn. Then just as quickly as it started it stops. Life has left his body and all that remains is a shell.

The spell on my mother is broken and she looks up from his bleeding body and towards me. I don't know what to say to her. Originally I had planned to kill her, to avenge my husband but after what we've just been through, I'm not sure it's a path I want to walk down anymore. Something in the air has shifted between us and whilst I can't say I forgive her yet, I can now see the benefit of having a relationship with her. Besides, she'd shocked me when she'd chosen me over Anton's promise to fund her movement. For a split second, I'd been so sure that would be a better prize for her than his death.

She leans over his body towards me, making a show of wiping her bloodied hands on her dripping trousers as she leans in and brushes a strand of hair from my face.

"It's over, my love."

Now that our mission is done apparently, so are the boundaries between us. The rain was slowing which I was grateful for, as much as the hood of Anton's jacket protected me the wind meant the occasional drop still brushed against my face. I dreaded to think how many fresh scars my skin would bear after tonight.

It had been worth it though. Anton was dead. The world was a marginally safer place. Now, all I had left to do was distribute the cure and I would have left to win against those formidable foes. Secondly, I now believe that truly in her heart, she thought the attack on the treatment centre was the right thing to do. She believed it would help make the world a better place, a fairer place, for me. I still resented her for choosing to stay in prison, for choosing to be a martyr, a figurehead over a mother but as a woman, I now understood her a little better.

"You never forgave me for destroying the treatment centre, did you?" Her gaze hardens slightly and my heart rate picks up under its intensity. My mother has never looked at me like this. Not even during our worst fights. Not even after I tried to kill her husband. I watch as her hand moves down towards her bag, expecting a nail to appear with my name on it. Instead what she pulls from inside makes my blood run cold.

The cure. My mother has the cure.
Before I can ask her anything the world around me goes black.

bypasses the reception team and calls my landline directly. I can tell because the ringtone is shriller than usual. There's only one person who has direct access to this line - Bailey.

"She's safe, for now," she assures me as soon as I pick up the receiver.

"Where is she?"

"She's going to be heading to the Waterfall this evening. To confront your father."

For a moment I'm lost for a response. A meeting between Paige and my father would not end well for either of them. Why couldn't she just wait until we could follow through with our original meet-up plan?

"Can you get a message to her?"

"It's too late for that. She's determined to do this."

"Maybe if I could talk to her?"

"Ryle -" she pauses and I know her next words will be meant with love but will sting nonetheless. "She won't listen to you. You don't mean as much to her as you think you do."

It wasn't true though. My Aunt didn't know what she was talking about. I knew my words could get through to Paige. To stop her from doing something catastrophic like starting a war she couldn't hope to finish. Bailey was wrong. Paige was my friend if nothing else. We'd forged a connection before all the lies were exposed. Hadn't we?

get out of hand. How has she pushed Paige into agreeing to this? Is she really going to use her daughter as bait to try and get to my dad? And would she succeed if she did?

My emotions were conflicting as my mind raced through all of the outcomes. Of who could live and who could die. But there was just one name that made my heart ache when I thought about never speaking it again - Paige. She had to live above anyone else. She'd survived too much to lose out on being reunited with her son when she was so close.

"I'm worried she's going to do something unforgivable." I wasn't sure if Bailey was referring to Paige or Di. "She's," she pauses and I can hear her clicking her tongue as she tries to work out what to say next. Was she about to share with me something she shouldn't?

"She's told me where to find Paige." It was an ominous use of words. Where to find Paige. It implies that Paige will be in a fixed location because she will be unable to move. Because she may be dead.

Bailey prided herself on being the keeper of secrets, so for her to divulge her conversation with Di to me, must mean that she had grave concerns.

"I haven't heard her this calm since the treatment centre." That confession from my aunt makes my skin crawl. The last time this woman was as calm as my aunt claims, a calamity of bloodshed soon followed. I

Oh God. Buried? She was going to bury her own daughter. She was walking Paige into a trap, under the guise that it was revenge against my father. She's treating her own child as collateral in her fight against the State. If my father gets his hands on Paige she won't stand a chance. He will snap her neck before he calls it into the authorities and explains it as an accidental fall.

No doubt he already has a press campaign prepared in one of the folders on his desk for that very scenario. My father liked to prepare for every possible outcome in life. By the morning I would be painted as the heartbroken widower. I couldn't let either of them end Paige's story mid-paragraph. She deserved to reach her finale. To disappear into the sunset with Franklin by her side.

"Thank you for letting me know."

"I'm sending some people over there now, but I don't know how much good they'll be if Di lashes out."

"Thank you. I'll speak to you later."

"Please make sure you do." So many unsaid things are laced into her parting sentence. Be careful. Good luck. I love you. Come home to us.

As I placed the receiver down my mind ticked over to the next problem at hand, how to lose the security guard that haunted my shadow?

make sure everybody knew they were mother and
daughter if she did anything to harm her. It would be
an unforgiveable sin, even in the eyes of her most
devout ally. I wanted everyone to know just how truly
insane she was.

But I couldn't make that call. I couldn't make use
of the resources my title leant me because if I did and
the wrong person attended the scene first, someone
in my father's pocket, then the outcome for Paige
would be the same. I was the only person I could
trust in this situation. It was up to me to stop the
events the three of them had set in motion. First
things first though, time to lose my security detail.

Today's shadow was called Clint. Clint wasn't as
chatty as my usual guard Barton but hopefully, that
would go in my favour. As I stepped into the corridor
he fell into rhythm just behind me. No small talk or
unnecessary chit-chat. I walked through the office,
making a show to stop and chat to the few workers
who had remained after hours, to help work on
various projects.

The head of accounts stopped me just before I
got in the lift and I happily signed the invoices he lay
before me. It was important that I wasn't in a rush. If
I seemed desperate to get out of the building then
Clint would pay more attention to my movements.
No matter how much I wanted to run to the ground
floor like a madman, I pushed the call button for the

assessing his physicality. I wasn't at my best in terms of physical strength so I would just have to hope that having a sense of purpose would give me an adrenaline boost. Like those parents who used to lift cars from their children. I need a dose of the unexplainable to help me overpower this man.

Now would be the perfect time to develop one of those mutations I'd heard so much about. I'd never witnessed one in real life. Even though I knew it would mean death would be on a ticking clock against me, it would mean I'd be able to help Paige. And, let's be honest, when wasn't death on a ticking clock against us? Briefly, I wondered if there were any samples in this building I could get my hands on, but with Clint by my side, I wasn't free to poke around.

We ride downstairs in the lift together in comfortable silence. He even briefly whistles a few bars from the tune he clearly has stuck in his head. He clears his throat when he realises what he's done and I know he'll be cursing himself for being unprofessional for the rest of our time together. I want to talk to him, to ask him what tune it was, when he first heard it and whether it had any significance to him. I wanted to connect with him emotionally on some level, after so many years of doing so it had become second nature to me. I couldn't do that though. If I humanised him, got to always bother him as little as possible with work requests, hoping in some way that this job could be almost like downtime to a man who never stops. Mentally I added his name to the list of employees I had to purchase a thank-you gift for. Maybe a voucher for a babysitting service and a nice restaurant so he and his wife could enjoy some time alone?

Here I was, making plans for a future I couldn't be certain of. If I arrived at the Waterfall and found someone about to hurt Paige what would I do? How far would I go to stop them? What if it were my father? Would I still be able to do what I felt needed to be done?

By now Clint is standing in front of my car door, holding it open for me and making a show of checking the perimeter around us. Thankfully we're alone. I move towards the open door and hold my hand out to shake his in thanks. He looks perplexed at this but not wanting to be impolite he mirrors my body language. Taking advantage of his change in stance, I turn my open hand into a fist and strike him below the chin. His head ricochets backward. It was a dangerous move on my part and could result in some permanent damage. But I'd been sure to keep my strike to a low level of movement. I only wanted to unbalance him not kill him.

Clint staggered backward, nearly losing his footing. One more move would be all I needed.

training kick in. He's going to jab me in the eyes to disable me if I let him. I jerk my head away from his hand without releasing my grip on his throat and slowly his body gives up the fight and sleep takes him.

I pulled him backward, shoving him haphazardly into the back seat of the car and slam it closed behind him.

"Computer engage locks." As a safety precaution since my father's punishment, this particular vehicle is only programmed to respond to my voice. By the time Clint wakes up and works out a way to get out of the car, I'll be long gone.

I wake up to the sound of sweating. My vision is blurry so whilst I wait for it to focus on the world around me, I note my physical state. My wrists are bound in front of me and I'm sat on my knees. A small wriggle of my ankles confirms my feet are also bound. I don't need to try and talk to realise there is a cloth hanging out of my mouth. God, I hope it's clean. I try to keep my breathing steady to hold off the panic but it's hopeless. My brain is already hyper-focused on my mortality, running through various scenarios of how this situation with my mother might play out.

She's kneeling in front of me, unaware that I am now conscious. I watch as she places rock after rock around my knees. I worry my heart is going to explode as I realise her plan - she's going to bury me alive.

I should never have turned to her for this mission. I should have learnt from her reaction to losing Kyan that she was a woman who didn't take kindly to her love being damaged. I'd tried to kill Jack. I'd robbed him of the personality she'd loved, and now she was going to seek her revenge. Naively, I'd thought the fact I was her own flesh and blood would save me from this fate. I should have known better. Nobody crosses my mother and lives to tell the tale.

I keep my eyes fixed on her as she adds more layers of rocks to the barricade in front of me. By now she is nearing my chest. It won't be long until I'm completely hidden from view, left to rot and wallow in my own misery before death comes for me. I grunt gently, wanting her to know that I am awake, that I am present.

Anton's body and their manhunt begins. How ironic that the mastermind they will be searching for will be buried mere feet from where their investigation will begin. Nobody else knows I've come here, there will be nobody to find my body.

I'll die and rot here behind these stones until my entrails break down and I become one with the waterfall. I suppose it's poetic in a way. My story started with a missed reservation here and it ends with a missed clue here. I should have known my mother better than this. She had been too obedient. Too willing to bend to my whim. I'd thought it was because she wanted my forgiveness, instead it was because she wanted my naivety.

At first, she tried to ignore the grunt I made but by now her hand is level with my chin as she continues placing rocks and stones in place. She has nowhere to look now other than straight into my eyes. I won't break eye contact. I won't be weak at this moment. I want her to remember the bond between us. To remember every childhood memory, every giggle as we ran with cheeky feet, every lesson she taught me and every night I fell asleep in her arms. She wasn't going to erase all of our memories to make this easier on herself. I wouldn't let her.

My death will mean something to her. No matter how hard she tries to fight it. I never dreamt we'd end up at this point, and despite her madness, I doubt my mother did either. What mother ever kills her child? Only one swept up in the insanity of their mind surely. I was? That she could end my story like this? I do not die like this, I will not die like this. I will escape and I will cure the Settlement and then I will finally be reunited with my son. My paragraph does not end mid-sentence. It won't. Despite my fury though, I am rather incapable of changing my current fate. Now the only part of me that is visible to the world is my face and she'll soon rid me of that freedom. I can see the cure, my cure, lying next to her bag at her feet as she selects the most secure-looking rocks.

"I never wanted it to come to this you know."

She has a captive audience at this moment, her favourite, so I prepare myself to hear her final monologue. Finally because as soon as I am free, I'll cut her tongue out before she can speak another word to me. I promise you Leo, I won't make the mistake of underestimating her again. I will kill her for what she did to you. What she did to us.

"There's a lot of things I regret about our life together, but this is probably the pinnacle of those" she chuckles to herself at her own dark sense of humour. "I regret the many moments that led to this. I have no choice you see. This is the only way to end it, I'm the only one who can end it."

Does she think that because she gave me life, she can take it as she pleases? I wouldn't be surprised to understand that was her logic.

She takes a deep breath and pauses in her task, two large rocks in her hands, the last two that will plunge me into darkness, until death comes for me.

involve putting myself directly in the firing line given the waterfall would soon swarm with agents. But it was the only way, it was impossible to reach the lake by the hospital so the lake at the bottom of the waterfall would be the next best option.

"I never apologised to you for the attack on the treatment centre did I? I never saw how much that choice affected you. I could only see my pain back then, it's only now that I've seen how you've grown, I realise how much my actions back then shaped you. I never should have gone that night. I was too angry to be rational. If I'd waited, I could have been smarter, perhaps less violent."

She smiles to herself at the memory of the blood she shed that night.

"Regardless, I could have achieved my aims without getting caught. Without becoming a martyr for my cause. I never should have risked my freedom when I had you to come home to. I'm sorry my darling."

Decades worth of tears are spilling down my cheeks. My head longs to be snuggled into her chest, to be held close and safe but I can't move. She's made sure I can't.

"I was selfish when I ordered Jack to attack Leo's car that night. For a start, I had no idea you and Franklin would be with him. I would never hurt you, Paige, I couldn't. But all I was thinking about was the benefits of the disease and its mutations. It had levelled the playing field between us and the State and I was terrified of losing ground without it. Once again, I put

She leans in through the barricade she's made around me and pushes a strand of hair back behind my ear, gently she wipes a tear from my eye.

"Please don't cry my darling, I've made you cry for enough lifetimes. You deserved a better mother than me. One less selfish and prone to flights of fancy. But oh, how I love you. I love you more than life itself little one. You are the very best part of me and I'm sorry I didn't see it when it mattered. You are going to change the world for the better Paige, I know you are and I can help you with this first step." She places one stone in front of my face, cutting my vision of the world in half. Don't leave me here mum. "You are my everything, Agapi Mou, please never forget that."

Her hand reaches through the small gap that remains and I fight against the restraint around my wrists. I have to break free and get to her. I try to speak under my gag but I know my words aren't clear. Please stay mum. I love you.

"This is the best way."

She reaches for me and traces the outline of my face as best she can. I can hear voices approaching in the distance, Anton's security has finally arrived. She has to get out of here. We can run together and talk, really talk to each other about all that we've been through. She has to give us that chance.

"I'll get the cure into the water. Bailey knows you are here."

She places her hand on her lips, kisses her fingertips, and places them on my forehead. Then darkness.

Mum, come back. We can fight them together. Please. Come back. Don't leave me, mummy.

There is a slither of light peeking in between the cracks in the stones and I move myself as best I can until my eye is pressed against it. The voices are louder now, they can only be feet away. I watch as my mother walks towards the edge of the waterfall, standing proudly over Anton's body as she clutches the pack of cures in her hands.

Throw them in and run Mum, you can make it. I know you can. I don't care if I have to go on the run because of this, it's not like I haven't spent the last two years hiding out. I'll make my way back to Franklin when the time is right, but this isn't the time Mum. This isn't your time.

I see the shadows of the guards approach, they pause as they take in the sight before them. I can see their guns raised in the air as they look down on their boss's body, on the empty shell of one of the Settlement's most powerful men. They all start shouting at once as they notice my mother's presence. She had to make sure she was seen so they wouldn't search for any other perpetrators. So they would have no reason to suspect me.

With a grace, I wasn't sure I knew she possessed she turns her back on the men and their shouts and takes two long strides towards the edge of the waterfall.

The space around her explodes in spurts of red as she's hit by their bullets. I have to hold in my screams and sobs as three pieces of soulless metal embed themselves in my mother. She was already falling by the time they punctured her skin and although I knew there would be no way for her to survive the fall from the top of the waterfall, I could have at least pretended had she not been riddled full of bullets the last time I lay eyes on her.

My natural instinct is to get to her, to save her in some way and I have to fight against myself to stay silent and still. She did all of this for me. She gave up her campaign against the State to ensure my safety. She chose me. She finally chose me.

Sweat was pouring down my face by the time I could see the Waterfall. Long distance running had never been my forte and I'd just spent a good couple of hours undertaking it, being sure to stick to side roads and paths less used. I couldn't afford to stop for a chat with a well-meaning citizen.

The storm had rolled in about half an hour ago, and the sound of the thunderclaps and the roar of the wind around me only gave me more motivation to reach the top of the waterfall in time to make a difference to Paige's fate. I couldn't let her mother or my father hurt her. The rain was beating down and I winced as I ran through its burning drops. At least when I looked back over these fresh scars, I'd know they'd been for a good purpose. They'd been to save my friend.

The lights in the restaurant are low, they're making the most of the natural light show around us. The lightning bolts that flash through the crowds light up the landscape around us and it's then that I notice the tiny figures picking their way up the side of the waterfall.

No.

I'm too late.

State Agents are here already.

The muscles in my legs protest loudly as I force them to pick up the pace. If I at least made it to the top just after them then I would serve as a witness. They couldn't act rashly with their President as a witness surely. There was still a chance I could stop them from undertaking my father's bidding.

or if I was just an oddity they'd tell their friends about in the morning.

The thunderclaps have slowed now and I almost miss them as silence overtakes the landscape around me. All I can hear is the struggling beats of my heart as it tries desperately to keep up with my adrenaline. This is not the time to quit. I'm so close.

The unmistakable sound of rapid gunfire shocks me to a stop.

No.

No.

This isn't possible. I have to be imagining this.

I look up towards the waterfall and that's when I see her falling. I fall to my knees as I realise I'm too late. The world swims to blackness as grief takes hold of me.

listened to the many voices just on the other side of the makeshift wall she'd hidden me behind as they discussed what had happened that day at the top of the waterfall.

How my mother had lured Anton from his table; he had after all, never mentioned my name to his security team, and brought him up here in the storm to torture and kill him. They figured it had been her ultimate act as the leader of the Anarchists to kill such a prominent political figure, although to the wider public, it would be reported as an innocent dentist, caught up in the whims of a mad woman.

His body wasn't moved immediately. I watched through the crack in my wall as an array of people and agents took their turns walking around him as he lay flayed out dead on the ground. His hatred is frozen in time. I was so detached from the situation though that I can't remember what any of them looked like, or even what gender they were. They were just faceless blobs swimming on the horizon. Eventually, though they moved his body and the cliff became quiet.

I heard his voice before I saw him. He asked the guards to leave him alone, telling them he would make his way home and that he needed some time alone to mourn and process what had happened. Frantically I tried shuffling around as best I could, desperate to let him know I was here. It took him ten minutes but eventually, he pulled me out of the cave and into his arms. Ryle held me with one arm as he used the other to cut the ties on my wrists and ankles. I didn't wince as once again, grief had me in its clutches. Eventually, though he lifted my head and wiped my face with his sleeve.

"Let's get you somewhere else shall we?"

His father's blood was on the floor at our feet and his only concern at that moment, was me. All the forgiveness he'd been longing for since the day of our wedding flushed through my body in that moment and I did something rather uncharacteristic.

I reached up with my aching hands and placed them on either side of his face. His eyes were tired and his warm features pinched with stress but his lips were turned up in the same gentle smile he flashed me when he first arrived into my life. Gently I leant forward and placed my lips on his. As I kissed him, I poured all the love and thanks I could manage into my touch and hoped it would reach his soul and help heal the wounds I knew he held deep inside. It's not your fault Ryle. None of it was your fault.

He pulls away from me after a while, breaking the one moment of true physicality between us in our relationship. Our faces remain so close our noses are touching and we spend a moment staring into each other's eyes. We are two humans who understand each other in a way no one else can. We both survived childhoods with parents who didn't prioritise us when we needed them most. We both spent most of our adult lives pretending to be something and someone we weren't, in order to appease society and we are both sick mountain together hand in hand. As we made our way down back to civilisation my mind drifted to Leo and Violet, back towards the life I'd lost. The loves I'd lost.

The actions of the night before with the deaths of my mother and Anton had gone some way to avenge their murders but there was still unfinished business out there. I drop Ryle's hand, if he notices then he makes no show of it. There are still things in this life that I need to do to make the world right.

****

Now I live in Dweller country with Rus, Theo, and my darling Franklin. I get to see him wake every morning and fall into a restful sleep every night. I get to offer him comfort when he falls and bangs his knee, or make him laugh with tickles and cuddles and watch him as he learns about the world around him. It's glorious and everything I'd longed for since the day they stole him from me.

We thought it sensible for me to move in with the three of them, to keep Franklin's life as stable as possible. I was after all, basically a stranger to him when I first arrived. Rus had of course told him about me every day and showed him my picture but he didn't truly remember me. It was easier for him to get used to me within the walls of the home he'd known for the last two years. He is getting used to me though. I'd like to think he remembers me, deep down inside, but I think he just remembers the idea of me. It's probably for the

Dwellers are still wary of my existence but thanks to Elijio, they know I helped put an end to the mutations on the battlefield. That I helped to right the wrong inflicted on their relatives.

It's been three months since Ryle dug me out of the cave my mother hid me in at the waterfall. Three months of peace, three months of sticky cuddles and childish giggles, three glorious months of settled happiness.

Georgia and Lizzie visit often. They live in my mother's sanctuary. The Anarchists are more of a political movement now than a radical one. I intend to join their ranks officially once Franklin is grown. I want to do something good with my mother's legacy. I owe her that after what she sacrificed for me but right now that isn't on the agenda.

The two of them are planning to get married soon and Georgia has asked me if I'll be a bridesmaid. I replied with a laugh and promised it would be less eventful compared to when she fulfilled that duty for me. It hurts less now to think of my wedding day and I'm able to see some humour in the absurdity of it all. I would never get over the way Violet was snatched from me but for now, the memories were softening at the edges at least, making them bearable to live with.

Violet was the only person in my life who had living memories of Leo. It's up to me alone to keep them alive now. I speak about him to Franklin a lot, though it makes little sense to my son. He doesn't really understand the concept of life and death yet and I the world is a very lucky place indeed.

I'm reading his favourite book to him as he sits on my lap cuddling into my chest, when the phone rings. I glance up at the clock, it's 6 p.m. The phone always rings at 6 p.m. Rus shoots me a knowing look that somehow manages to be both irritating and charming and scoops Franklin out of my arms. My son briefly protests but gives in pretty quickly when faced with a bout of tickles to the belly. I let the phone ring a few more times as I enjoyed the sound of his giggle. I don't think I'll ever tire of that sound. I take a deep breath and reach for the receiver.

"Hello Miss Joseph," his voice is light with his sense of humour.

He changes the name he greets me with every evening. Explaining that I'm a woman of many talents and to assign that to just one name would be criminal. I can't help but laugh, the same way I do at this time every day. He's never late for these calls and I always enjoy them. What started originally as Ryle checking to see how I was settling in, evolved into a nightly ritual we both looked forward to. Our conversations rarely went deeper than the actions of our day but still, I relished the snippets of office gossip he shared with me and I know he meant every laugh as I told him about the latest piece of mischief Franklin had got himself into.

One of the few times our conversation was deeper than usual was when Ryle informed me he had relinquished all parental rights of Franklin back to me. The State no longer had any hold over my son. I was so about the infection of the Settlement.

We spoke about our shared experiences sometimes. It helped us to process the last few years but more often than not, we liked to live in the present. Ryle is still President, except now he doesn't have to answer to his father. He isn't exactly free to do as he wishes but the reins are getting looser every day. One day he'll achieve everything he wanted to, and it will be the most celebrated day in human history. He just has to keep a wary eye on the power of the remaining members of the Téssera.

They have yet to rear their heads and meet him in person but he's explained to me that their influence is everywhere. Sometimes, after an impassioned speech to the nation, he can tell he's being followed home. It's their way of warning him they can dispose of him when they see fit.

Unfortunately for them, he's the most popular politician in all of living history. His numbers in the polls outstrip any President on this Earth or the last. Anton's plan to have him marry the great Dr Paige has been a little too successful, the public is still swooning over our fictional love story. Me kidnapping him and threatening to destroy the human race just added to the star-crossed lover's appeal - especially since Ryle has been working overtime to clear my name and reputation in the public sphere.

That's one thing we never talk about though - our marriage. Neither of us seems able to find the words to put our thoughts and feelings about it into a coherent while, a dangerous level of determination glinting behind her pupils. It can mean only one thing. We finally have another name. She nods at me to confirm my suspicions and waits for my response, waiting for me to agree to the next hunt.

I can hear Ryle's voice as he reaches the end of a sentence. I'd almost forgotten he was at the other end of the line. With a soft chuckle, he realises my attention was elsewhere and asks "Penny for your thoughts?"

A lifetime of happy memories floods through my head as I reply on instinct, "Worth more than a cent I'm afraid."

The End

I'll be a bit more organised and everything won't be a sprint.

Everytime I embark on the madness that is writing and publishing a book I realise how lucky I am to have the village I do behind me – Mum, Charlotte, Viv, Liz and Dobsy, none of this would be possible without your support and red pens!

My editor Allison, who also happens to be one of my closest friends now, is a true talent at making my words sparkle and shine. I recommend her to anyone and everyone.

Sophie Linfield, the woman who in my mind has become Paige through and through – two audiobooks down just one more to go! We'll have to come up with a new project to give us an excuse for endless voice notes now!

Finally thank you to you, the reader, if you've made it this far through Paige's journey then I applaud you. Hopefully you've enjoyed the ride and have finally forgiven me for what I did to Leo!

Reviews really do make or break a book, especially an indie book so please do consider leaving a rating or a review wherever you purchased this novel. Thank you for taking even more time out of your life to spend in one of my worlds.

Steph is currently working on a number of standalone psychological thriller books which will start to be released in 2024.

For updates and pre-order notifications on future publications please consider signing up to the mailing list or following SM Thomas on your platform of choice.